House in Motion

Lucky was still asleep when he heard a noise. It was like a huge truck, or maybe a train. And someone was shaking Lucky's bed. "Don't," Lucky said. Dad or Grandma, or someone, was rocking his bed back and forth, making it flop around like a hammock.

Suddenly Lucky was awake. He was hearing crashing noises. Things were falling. Glass was breaking. And still his bed was rolling. Lucky thought something had hit the house—the truck he had heard, or maybe a tree had fallen.

And then he knew.

"Earthquake!" he yelled, although he didn't know who could hear him.

BOOKS BY DEAN HUGHES

From Deseret Book

The Lucky books: Lucky's Crash Landing;
Lucky Breaks Loose; Lucky's Gold Mine;
Lucky Fights Back; Lucky's Mud Festival;
Lucky's Tricks; Lucky the Detective;
Lucky's Cool Club; Lucky in Love;
Lucky Comes Home

The Williams family historical novels:
Under the Same Stars; As Wide as the River;
Facing the Enemy; Cornbread and Prayer

Other titles: Brothers; Hooper Haller; Jenny Haller;
The Mormon Church, a Basic History; Great Stories
from Mormon History (*with Tom Hughes*)

From other publishers

The Nutty books:
Nutty Can't Miss; Nutty Knows All;
Nutty, the Movie Star; Nutty's Ghost; Reelect Nutty

Angel Park All-Stars, numbers 1–14

Angel Park Soccer Stars, numbers 1–8

Angel Park Hoop Stars, numbers 1–4

Other titles:
Jelly's Circus; Theo Zephyr; Family Pose
(*paperback titled* Family Picture); End of the Race;
Baseball Tips (*with Tom Hughes*)

LUCKY
COMES HOME

DEAN HUGHES

CINNAMON
TREE ®

Published by
Deseret Book Company
Salt Lake City, Utah

For Garth and Ann Pierce

Library of Congress Cataloging-in-Publication Data

Hughes, Dean, 1943–
    Lucky comes home / Dean Hughes.
        p.   cm.
    "Cinnamon Tree."
    Summary: When his father is nearly killed in the aftermath of an earthquake, the incident helps Lucky accept the possibility that his father may remarry.
    ISBN 0-87579-941-8
    [1. Fathers and sons—Fiction. 2. Remarriage—Fiction. 3. Earthquakes—Fiction. 4. Mormons—Fiction.] I. Title.
PZ7.H87312Luc   1994
[Fic]—dc20   94-30762
                                                                                CIP
                                                                                AC

Printed in the United States of America

10   9   8   7   6   5   4   3   2   1

Chapter 1

As Lucky entered the airport terminal, he spotted his grandparents. And Grandma spotted Lucky. She broke into a run, her arms spread wide. Lucky thought for a moment that she might run right over him. She stopped just in time, sweeping him off his feet and spinning him around. "You're home at last," she squealed. "And home to stay."

Lucky's legs swung in a wide arc. His foot hit a woman in the shins—which drew a complaining grunt—but Grandma didn't seem to notice. She dropped Lucky onto his feet and moved to her son—Lucky's dad. She had to jump to throw her arms around his neck.

Lucky was a little embarrassed at Grandma's wild behavior in front of so many people. But then, that was Grandma Ladd. He liked her the way she was. She was wearing a brilliant red sweat suit with a matching headband. Her hair, dyed dark as always, was in a ponytail.

Ron Ladd clung to Grandma a long time, and then he pulled her under one big shoulder while he grabbed Grandpa, who had now approached. Dad hugged both of them at the same time, one in each arm. When he finally stepped back a little, he said, "Remember, Mom, I didn't *promise* we were home for good. I only said we were thinking in that direction."

"Well, don't start thinking anything else. I won't hear of it."

Dad grinned. "What in the world are you wearing?" he asked.

"I have to go to my aerobics class the very minute we get back."

"That's just an excuse," Grandpa said. "That's what she wears all the time now. *Sweat suits.* She looks like she's going around in pajamas all day."

Grandma gave Grandpa a little slug on the shoulder, and then she winked at Lucky's dad. Gesturing along the lines of her thin body, she said, "He just hates this outfit because it's red. He hates anything red. He calls this my University of Utah suit."

Grandpa was smiling a little. But he rolled his eyes in mock disgust. "Hey, you cheer for Utah all the time. You know you do."

"That's right. Every game. Except when they play BYU. What's wrong with that?"

Grandpa shook his head. Though he didn't say anything, his look said, "If you don't know, how can I explain it to you?"

Grandma had lost interest in the subject, however. She had focused on Lucky again. "What's in the sack?" she asked. "Something for me?"

"Oh, sorry. Yeah, it is for you." Lucky had momentarily forgotten about the lei he had brought her.

"Good!" Grandma didn't wait for Lucky to hand it over. She reached into the sack and pulled out a lei in a plastic container. "I knew you'd bring me a lei!" She draped the white and yellow plumeria flowers around her neck. "It looks good with my sweat suit, don't you think?" She nudged Grandpa with her elbow.

Grandpa mumbled, "You mean your pajamas."

Grandma paid no attention. She grabbed Lucky's duffle bag from his hand. "Come on, let's go get your luggage." After three long steps, which caught the others off guard, she slowed and waited for them. "Lucky, you *are* home for good now. Don't let your dad start dragging you all around the world anymore. Just say *no*—like with drugs."

"Dad says we might stay here for a couple of months, and then see what—"

"Don't listen to him. He's only your father. You're

going to live with us for a while. And then you're going to buy a house. *Orrrrrrr* . . . there's already a nice house in our neighborhood, with a *very* nice lady in it. And that lady could use a *very* nice husband and a *lovely* new son."

On and on she talked, telling Lucky and his dad how wonderful it would be if they lived in her ward, just a block or so away. Lucky's cousins were nearby, too, and everyone could get together "all the time." To her, it all sounded perfect.

Lucky had steeled himself for this. The last time he and his dad had spent a little time in Provo, Grandma had introduced Dad to a woman—Carol Wakefield. Back then, Dad had said he wasn't ready to remarry. He was still too attached to Lucky's mother, who had died of cancer. But during these past few months, with Lucky and his dad on the road again, Lucky could tell that his dad missed Carol.

So Dad had come home to make a decision. Lucky had even vowed to accept whatever happened. But it wasn't easy. And now Grandma was making it all sound so settled.

An image—one he had visualized many times— passed through Lucky's mind. He saw himself in the Wakefields' house. He was eating breakfast, sitting at their kitchen table, and he was surrounded by people he didn't really know. It was strange and uncomfortable and . . . impossible. He just hated the idea.

Whenever Lucky told himself he would have to deal with it, and therefore *could* deal with it, Tyler would come to mind. Tyler was Carol's son, the same age as Lucky. And he was a mess. The kid had been through some hard experiences. His father had walked out on the family, without warning, and then later had told Tyler he was in love with another woman. Tyler was angry and confused. Lucky understood that, and he could tolerate the kid, but the thought of having him for a brother made Lucky shudder.

Somewhere halfway down the moving sidewalk in the Salt Lake airport, Grandpa finally came to Lucky's rescue. "Lucky, how was your flight?" he asked, and he actually pulled Lucky back a step so that he was out of Grandma's direct range.

"Kind of long," Lucky said.

"The drive back to Provo could get a little long too," Grandpa whispered. He glanced at Grandma, and then he winked at Lucky. Grandma had started in on Lucky's dad now. She was telling him that Carol was prettier than ever. "And I *know* she's missed you since you left."

Lucky heard his dad say, "Mom, you ought to know by now, this is not the right approach with me." He was smiling, but he sounded firm.

Things went better in the car. Even Grandma seemed to know that she had pushed too hard. Lucky's mood was ruined, though. During the flight his thoughts had stayed in Hawaii. He had felt sad to leave, but he was still filled with the glow of all that had happened to him there. Now, he realized, the decision about Carol was going to come, and maybe it was going to come much more quickly than he had expected. Worse than that, he was sure he knew what the decision would be.

What Lucky really wished was that he and his dad could just get into their RV and head out on the road again. For over two years, since Lucky's mother had died, the two of them had been moving every few weeks. Dad worked for an insurance company, and he had been in charge of setting up emergency headquarters where disasters had happened. Lucky and his dad were each other's whole world, and Lucky liked it that way.

Lucky looked out the window while Dad told his parents about the devastation the hurricane had done in Maui. Lucky thought, however, that Utah was what looked devastated. Lucky had never realized how colorless the mainland was. It was early May, really one of the prettiest times in Utah, but he had just left a place that was fifty shades of green—an island wrapped up in blue sky and blue water. Now he saw stark mountains, granite gray. He had always liked the mountains, but they looked like walls now. Someone needed to give them a good paint job.

Still, Lucky felt a little better when he saw the old neighborhood on Provo's Grandview Hill. At Grandma's house he was glad to see his motor home parked in the driveway. He wished he were sleeping in it that night. That would seem more like coming home.

The sight of his cousin Willy sitting on Grandma's front steps cheered Lucky even more. Willy stood up and thrust his hands in the air, as though he had just scored a touchdown and he was now accepting the applause of a vast crowd. The day was blustery, not really all that warm, but Willy had on a baggy pair of shorts and a T-shirt about seven sizes too big. Across the front was printed "REMEMBER, DOGS ARE PEOPLE TOO," whatever that meant. Willy didn't even have a dog.

His cousin loped to the car and waited for Lucky to open the door. "You're home, Lucky. It's going to be great, man. It's going to be *wet* and *wild* and *wonderful*."

Lucky laughed. He had no idea what would be wet and wild, but then, Willy spoke his own language.

"Your only problem will be that all the girls around here are already in love with me, so you won't stand a chance. You're a good guy, Lucky, but let's face it, you're ugly to the bone."

Lucky surveyed Willy. The guy was tall and thin, made out of crooked bones, it seemed. His teeth were too big for his mouth. His hair, stuffed under a beat-up, old baseball cap, was sticking straight out over his ears. "Well, Willy, you ought to know something about ugly. You look at it in the mirror every day."

"Yeah. That's right. I gotta stop my sisters from looking over my shoulder all the time."

Now that was a good one. Willy raised his hands in triumph again and began to make a sound like a one-cylinder engine chugging at a revved-up pace—the famous Willy laugh.

He stopped laughing just as suddenly as he had begun and said, "Hey, let's get your stuff inside. Then we've got some things we've got to do."

Lucky had no idea what had to be done, though he sort of liked the idea of taking off with Willy. His spirits took a big leap.

Then Dad said, "Don't run off, Lucky. I want you to go with me somewhere."

Lucky couldn't believe it. There was only one place they would be going to that quickly. Dad had brought leis for Carol and her daughters. Lucky hadn't thought *he* would have to go over there, at least not for a while.

Still, go he did. He and his dad unpacked first,

while Willy hung around. Then, after Dad took a quick shower and put on his new Hawaiian shirt, Lucky and his dad took the leis, and they walked around the corner and down the block to the Wakefield house.

No question about it—the Wakefields were waiting. Maybe Dad had called first. Lucky wasn't sure. They were spit-shined and done up beautiful. The daughters—Kristin, Heather, and Molly—all beamed as Dad put leis around their necks. And Carol laughed and said, "I thought a person was supposed to get a kiss with one of these."

That was true. That's how it was always done. Lucky knew that. But he had never seen his dad kiss a woman before—not since his mom had died.

Dad did it sort of playfully—just a tiny peck on her cheek. Carol, with her fair skin, turned red all the way to her blonde hair. Lucky thought she sounded like a teenager, the way she giggled.

The girls teased her too. Heather, who was nine, shouted, "Wooo-wooo. None of that stuff, Mom. Not in front of us kids."

Kristin, who was sixteen, said, "I thought you told *me* not to kiss guys."

Molly was laughing in her low little voice, and Dad began to emit rolls of laughter that shook the house like a thunderstorm.

Lucky was the only one not laughing. Or at least

that's what he thought. About then he stepped a little farther down the front hallway and saw Tyler sitting on the living-room couch. Tyler was staring straight ahead. He looked as though he wanted to hit someone.

Lucky might have felt some kinship in that, but that's not what he felt at all. Lucky knew who Tyler wanted to slug. It was Lucky's dad—the guy kissing his mother.

By the time the whole group had migrated to the living room, Dad had taken some big-time teasing about his Hawaiian shirt. Finally he got a chance to greet Tyler. "Hey, Tyler, I thought about bringing you a lei too, but I figured you wouldn't want one. And I didn't have room in my suitcase for a surfboard."

He laughed, but Tyler didn't. Tyler stared coldly at Mr. Ladd, as if to say, "I'm not going to pretend that I like you."

Dad sort of sputtered for words. "Ol' Lucky got to be a real expert at surfing while we were over there," he said. "Maybe he can give you some lessons out on Utah Lake."

Dad laughed again, but not as loudly as usual. Tyler continued to stare at him. The room had gotten very quiet.

"Did you really learn to surf, Lucky?" Carol finally asked.

"I tried. I wiped out most of the time. You can still

see where I banged up my face." The scratches and scabs were gone, but a patch of skin over his eye and a streak along one cheek were lighter than the rest of his face. Lucky always thought of himself as a rather goofy-looking kid, what with his glasses and his buck teeth and braces. He hated to have all these girls staring at him. Still, Tyler's cold stare was worse than any of that.

"You really did scrape yourself up, didn't you?" Carol said, reaching out and touching his cheek.

Something about that bugged Lucky. It was as though she wanted to act "motherly." And Lucky hadn't come over to the Wakefields to look for a mother.

Chapter 2

Lucky didn't last long at the Wakefields. Tyler got up and left the room—and didn't return. Lucky hung in there for another fifteen minutes or so, listening to Dad's accounts of Maui and hearing what the girls had been doing lately. Finally he said, "Dad, Willy wanted me to come over."

Dad started to protest, but Carol quickly said, "Oh, go ahead, Lucky. I know this can't be very fun for you."

"Well, no . . . it's okay. I just wanted to see Willy for a while."

Lucky could see that his dad was disappointed in how this get-together had gone, but Lucky slipped out anyway. And on the way to Willy's he told himself that Tyler had been the jerk. Lucky couldn't do much if the guy wouldn't even try to be friendly. The kid had actually gotten sort of friendly when Lucky had been home in January—once he knew that Lucky and his dad were leaving. Now, though, he wouldn't even try to act human. So why should Lucky make any effort?

Somewhere in the back of Lucky's mind was also the idea that maybe Dad would see that this whole thing just wasn't going to work. And that thought, whether Lucky admitted it or not, relieved him a little.

Lucky hung around with Willy for a while and then told him that he'd better be heading back to Grandma's house.

"Why?" Willy asked. "Your dad's going to be over there kissing Sister Wakefield for a long time yet."

"Shut up."

"Grandma says they'll be married before the summer is over." Willy was lying on his back on his bedroom floor, with his hands behind his head.

"Yeah, but Grandma isn't the one to decide. It's my dad. And he told me already, he's not going to rush into anything." Lucky wasn't entirely sure he believed that himself, but he liked the sound of it.

"Hey, I think it'll be great. You'll live right here in the neighborhood. Tyler's a geek, but who cares? As long as you get your own room, you can just avoid him and hang out with me all the time. I'll get you on my soccer team."

"I don't know how to play soccer."

"Okay, I'll explain it. You kick a ball. And then you

kick it again. If you get a chance, you kick it in a net. But the goalie's always in the way. So you only make a goal about once every two centuries. It's the boringest game ever invented."

"Then how come you play?"

"Well, I'll explain that too—since you asked." He pulled his hands out from under his head and swung them wide apart in a gesture that had nothing to do with anything—except that Willy always made gestures like that. "When I play baseball, I don't get any hits, see." He nodded and waited for Lucky to respond.

"Okay, but you said—"

"Now wait. Think about this. I don't get hits, but other guys do. And if I play basketball, I don't make baskets, but once again, other guys do. Now . . . if I play soccer, I don't score, but neither does anyone else—at least not very often. And that means no one can tell how lousy I am."

"You still know."

"Who cares? At least I can tell Erin and Celeste that I play. And I don't look like some goofus who can't play any sports."

"Who are Erin and Celeste?"

"My girlfriends."

"Two of them?"

"Why not? The nice thing is, they don't understand soccer, so they don't know if I'm lousy or not."

"So do these girls both like you?"

"Good question." For some reason, Willy suddenly made a chopping motion with his hand above his face. "I'd have to say, if they do like me, they're keeping their emotions very well hidden. But then"—and he swung his arms wide again—"girls are like that sometimes."

"I thought girls usually made it pretty clear if they liked you."

"Don't judge by what you see Sister Wakefield doing. She's after your dad."

"Willy, lay off. Okay? Dad already told me he won't marry her unless I feel good about it."

"Hey, I'd love it—living over there. I could stare at Kristin as long as I wanted to. I could put in about three hours a day at that and never get tired."

"Kristin's really nice, Willy. She's the best thing about that family."

"Hey, did I say she wasn't nice? She just happens to be very nice to look at."

"Willy, she'd be my sister. Sort of, anyway. I couldn't just sit around and stare at her." Lucky was sitting on Willy's bed, looking down at Willy.

"Well, that's true. I'll tell you what. I'll come over to your house and stare for you. She won't be my sister." Willy began to chug away with his weird laugh.

Lucky smiled too. But he didn't want to think about

that situation anymore—and he especially didn't want to talk about it. He was also very tired. He decided to leave and get to bed early.

As he walked to Grandma's, he hoped that his dad would be back home—that he hadn't stayed at the Wakefields too long. The worst thought of all was that his dad and Sister Wakefield really were over there sitting on the couch, the kids all gone now, kissing each other—like two stupid teenagers on a date. The whole idea made Lucky cringe.

What would Lucky's mom think of Dad doing stuff like that?

When Lucky got to Grandma's house (he never thought of it as Grandpa's house), he found what he feared. Dad was still gone. Grandma told Lucky to come into the kitchen and have some dinner. She had kept a plate warm for him. When Lucky started to eat, she sat down by him. "Well, Lucky, your dad has been over at Wakefields' a *long* time. Those two must have a lot to talk about." She flashed a big smile, as though she were doing a toothpaste commercial.

Lucky didn't like that. He didn't say anything, and he didn't smile back at her.

"What's wrong, Lucky?" Grandma asked.

"Nothing."

"I thought you'd be excited to have a family. Your dad told me you were getting used to the idea."

Lucky didn't know how to answer. He thought for a time and finally said, "I guess it's up to him. I'm not getting much choice in the whole thing."

"Well, sure, it's up to him. But aren't you happy for him?"

"Yup. I've never been so happy in my whole life."

Grandma leaned forward so she was staring right into his face. She seemed serious for once. "Lucky, come on. We've talked about this before. You don't want him to be alone the rest of his life, do you? You'll be gone in a few years, and he won't have anyone."

"I know."

"I talked to your other grandma—your mother's mother. And she feels the same way."

Lucky was interested to hear that. He had been curious to know how she felt. She and Grandpa Nielson were in St. George at their condo. They would be coming back before too much longer, Dad had said, and Lucky wanted to talk to them about all this. He supposed he only wanted them to be on his side, and it didn't sound as if they would be.

The truth was that, more than anything, Lucky hated all the changes that would come. How could he just move in with a whole new family? All those girls? How could he deal with Tyler? How could he let Carol start acting like she was his mother? "Grandma, I don't know . . . " But he didn't even know how to finish his sentence.

"It'll be a big change. But those girls are all so sweet. They'll all love you to death. And Tyler will grow out of this thing of his—you know, his anger and hurt. I know you two can like each other."

Lucky didn't want to talk about a new family. So he finished his dinner and hid away in his room, which had once been his dad's when he was growing up in this house. The first thing Lucky did was find his mom's picture that he had carried with him in his duffle bag. He put the picture on the dresser by the bed. He wanted it close, where he could see it. That's what he told himself. But he knew the truth. He wanted to force his dad to look at it.

Lucky didn't get in bed yet but lay back on the pillow, on top of the bedspread, with his clothes on. The next thing he knew, he was hearing the door open. He sat up, a little confused, and then realized that he had drifted off to sleep. His dad was standing in the doorway, still holding the doorknob, just sort of peeking in.

"Lucky, you'd better get into bed. You're wiped out."

Lucky nodded, his mind still full of cobwebs. As he slid his legs off the side of the bed and then sat for a moment, Dad stepped into the room. "Can I talk to you for just a minute?"

Lucky nodded again. He knew what was coming, and he didn't want to hear it.

"Carol and I had a really good talk. We've decided there's no way we can get married, the way things are right now. Who knows? Maybe some day in the future. But not for now. So you can stop worrying about it."

Lucky was awake now. And stunned. His first impulse was relief, but he had heard the tone in his dad's voice. Dad was standing like a giant high above Lucky, but his hands were in his pockets, and his face was empty. His eyes looked dead.

"How come?"

"It just isn't going to work right now. I guess Tyler is the biggest problem. But it would be hard for everyone."

Lucky heard the flatness in his dad's voice. It was the way he had sounded so often after Mom had died. Lucky hated that memory, feared that his dad would have to go through another time like that. And he was struck with guilt. "Is it because of me, too?"

"Well, you're not happy about it. I know you always try to make the best of things, but I don't like forcing you into something you obviously don't want."

Lucky didn't know what to say. He was already ashamed for the things he had been thinking all day. Yet he couldn't bring himself to say that he was willing to move in with the Wakefields.

When Lucky looked up again, he saw that his dad had spotted the picture on the dresser. Dad didn't step closer, but he stood looking at it for quite some time. "Lucky," he said, and that terrible flatness was still in his voice, "I wish more than anything that your mom were still here. That would be the best. But we didn't get that choice."

"I know."

"The only question is what I should do now that we don't have what we want. Carol had a good marriage once, but then her husband seemed to forget who he was. If she could go back to the way things were, that's what she would want too."

Lucky nodded.

"Whatever we do, it'll only be second best, at best. Actually, for right now, I suppose second best is sticking with things the way they are."

"Will we stay here—or start traveling again?"

"I don't know. You and I need to talk about that."

But Lucky didn't know how to talk about it. He liked the idea of getting back in the RV and heading out. He'd gotten used to fresh starts. For a long time he hadn't had to stick anything out for more than a month or so.

It was the laughter, though, the fun he and his dad had always shared—that's what made it all work. He didn't want to drive away if his dad's eyes were going to look that way. For the first time what Lucky needed wasn't what his dad needed, and Lucky didn't know what to do about that.

"Dad, it's okay with me if you marry her. I'll be okay about it."

When Lucky looked up again, his dad was smiling, sadly. They had both heard the tone in Lucky's voice this time. It was as though he had said, "Go ahead and do something terrible. I'll live with it somehow."

"Lucky, I know you'd be okay about it. And after a while I really think you might be happy with the whole situation. But I don't know that for sure. And Carol doesn't either. Right now we feel like our number-one responsibility has to be to you kids. We're not a couple of kids falling in love. We have to think about the whole situation."

Lucky felt a pain stab at him—partly for what he was causing his dad to say, but also for that awful word his dad had used. Did Dad really love her? How could he do that to Mom?

Dad seemed to sense what Lucky was thinking. He was looking at the picture again. Lucky looked at his mom too. The picture had been taken when Mom was quite young, before she got cancer, before she got so pale and worn out. She was smiling, looking pleased and relaxed, happy. The truth was, Lucky couldn't remember her like that. He remembered her as quiet

and determined, even funny at times, but always soft-
ened by the knowledge that she was dying.

"We'll stick around here for a while," Dad said,
"and we'll talk things over. Figure out what's best.
Okay?"

Lucky couldn't answer. Every answer he could
think of was wrong. Dad patted him on the head with a
hand the size of a baseball glove, and then he walked
to the door. He stopped there and looked back. "We'd
better not stay with Grandma too long. Her cooking
will kill us off."

That was true. Grandma really was a rotten cook.
She specialized in overcooking everything. "Just scrape
that black stuff off the chicken," she had told him when
she gave him his dinner. But the "black stuff" had gone
pretty deep, and the chicken was dry as cardboard.
Dad's famous Shake 'n' Bake chicken was a whole lot
better.

"Good idea," Lucky said, and he tried to smile.

Dad even laughed, but he couldn't seem to get his
usual power into it. The light fixture rattled a little, but
it didn't shatter and fall to the floor.

Dad left, and in another minute Lucky could hear
his big, deep voice out in the living room. He was talking softly, and Lucky could only pick up the vibrations.
But he knew that he was telling his parents that he

wasn't getting married. He knew too that Grandma was going to be sad for her son.

Lucky just sat on the edge of his bed and stared straight ahead. He couldn't think what was right. And he couldn't look at the picture of his mom. Lucky knew what she had said. When she was dying, right at the end, she had told Dad he needed to get married again, that he and Lucky shouldn't be alone. But Lucky never had been able to understand that. How could he and his dad be alone when they were together?

Chapter 3

Lucky and his dad had agreed to talk, but they didn't do it. The next day Dad told Lucky, "We'll get this all figured out one of these days. For now, we'd better get you into school." So Lucky enrolled at Grandview Elementary. As far as he knew, he would finish out the few weeks of the school year there.

While Dad went to work every day at the local office of the insurance company, Lucky went to school. Dad didn't say anything about buying a house. And Grándma stopped talking about the Wakefields almost entirely. Lucky figured Dad had told her that's what he wanted.

Lucky really didn't know how to deal with his situation. He had worked out a sort of routine for handling things each time he started at a new school. In his previous moves, he had always known he would be around for only a few weeks, and he had acted accordingly. For one thing, he always tried to locate any local Mormons. That often helped him find a friend. In Provo, however, he could throw a rock in any direction and hit a Mormon. But then, so could everyone else. So there was no special tie to anyone.

His other trick was to pick someone who seemed to need a friend, and then he would offer to get acquainted. That had always been easy. The nice thing was, if he met some guy he really didn't like all that much, he wasn't around long enough for it to matter much. But now he felt he needed to fit in with some group at the school and stick.

The good news was, Lucky was not in the same sixth-grade class with Tyler. And he was in the same class with Willy, though that quickly became a bit complicated. Word soon got back to Lucky that Tyler was going around telling everyone that Lucky was a real doofus. Lucky hoped that kids would consider the source, but the trouble was, Willy was considered a bit of a doofus himself. And Willy never seemed to leave Lucky's side.

It was sort of the same at church. Seeing the same kids at church whom he saw at school every day was strange for Lucky. He liked the fact that he knew most of the guys in his deacons quorum, since he had met them the previous winter, but once again there was

Tyler whispering to the guys, probably saying the same kind of stuff he was saying at school.

There was also Willy being Willy—always ranging somewhere from a little weird to very weird. Most of the guys seemed to like him, basically, but that was because they had known him all their lives, and they accepted him for who he was. Lucky couldn't be Willy, and he wasn't sure whether he could find some way to be accepted for himself. No one—except Tyler— seemed to have anything against him, but Lucky still wasn't sure where he was going to fit in—and Tyler was making things as difficult for him as he could.

Willy did keep one promise. He got Lucky on his soccer team. From all appearances, however, that was not a tough trick to pull off. Lucky had the impression that once the other coaches had chosen the players they wanted, the leftover guys had been organized into a team of their own—the Weasels.

"The what?" Lucky had asked.

"Hey, I thought it up," Willy told him. "Weasels are mean little critters."

So Lucky was now a Weasel, dressed in a uniform that had once been maroon but now was faded to a color way too close to pink for Lucky's liking. And the coach made him a fullback. The only thing Lucky understood about the position was that he should stay fairly close to his own goal and "play tough defense," as the coach put it. Lucky figured it was like being put in right field in baseball. The coach knew enough to put his weak guys in a place where he hoped they couldn't do too much damage.

Actually, Lucky spent most of his time in an even safer place: on the sidelines watching the other guys play.

Then one afternoon, with the game already lost, the coach said, "Ladd, I'm going to let you play the second half. You need the experience." Lucky was sort of pleased, since sitting on the sidelines was so boring, but he couldn't get too excited with the other team—the Sasquatches—leading 8 to 0.

All the same, he trotted onto the field and took up his position for the kickoff. "We can still beat these guys," Willy yelled.

Yeah, right.

Willy had said the same thing before the game. He had called the other team the "Big Foots" and claimed they all had arms that reached to their knees. All Lucky had seen so far, however, were fast feet.

But that was better than what he saw when play started in the second half. (And seeing wasn't his strong point right now, since Lucky had taken his glasses off.) The Sasquatches moved the ball quickly toward the Weasels' goal, and Lucky found himself trying to mark a guy whose knees were about the same elevation as Lucky's nose. The player was a boy named Crump—with no apparent first name—and everyone said he was the best player in the league.

Lucky got after the guy, however, and when a Sasquatch kicked a pass in Crump's direction, Lucky darted in and kicked the ball away.

Crump didn't like that.

The Sasquatches came back quickly on attack. This time the king of the Sasquatches dropped back and took a pass. Then he charged hard toward the goal. Lucky stepped in front of him and cut off his path.

He thought.

It turned out the path to the goal, in this case, went *over* Lucky instead of around him.

When the world stopped spinning, Lucky realized he was on his back, while the Sasquatches were performing a tribal victory dance—the same one he had seen eight times before (from a better position).

Willy ran to Lucky and hauled him to his feet. "Are you okay?" he shouted. "Where are you hurt?"

Lucky was hurting in several places, actually, and it was hard to say which of the spots would eventually turn out to be the winner.

Then Willy said, "Oh, man, your mouth is bleeding. *Bad*."

It was the old smash-your-braces-into-your-lip injury. The coach had told Lucky he needed a mouthpiece. Lucky just hadn't figured it would be that important to have one—on the sidelines.

So about forty seconds into the second half, Lucky's playing time was over. The coach found a towel, and Lucky sat down in his familiar spot. He didn't really mind being out of the game, but he wasn't too excited about the way his lip was swelling.

"Just wait until the game is over, and then I'll walk you home," Willy told Lucky.

Lucky actually would have preferred to walk on home sooner than that, but he agreed to hang around. So he lay back on the grass and rested, trying to get the bleeding to stop.

The day was really nice, warmer than it had been since Lucky and his dad had arrived. The air was clear, and the mountains were standing tall. Lucky was starting to remember why he liked Utah, and by now he wasn't constantly comparing it to Hawaii. The warmth and the blue sky, with only a few splotches of clouds overhead, were very calming.

Lucky shut his eyes and thought of the beach at Kaanapali. Even his banged-up face brought back memories. He thought of the other face too—her face. Kaahu. He wondered what she was doing now. He had written to her once, but he hadn't received an answer yet. "Ka-a-hu," he whispered to himself. He loved the sound of her name.

"Oh, oh. Lucky's talking to himself. Maybe he is weird."

Lucky opened his eyes. Two girls stepped a little closer. The afternoon sun was angling from behind them, and he couldn't see who they were. He sat up.

"Who wouldn't be weird with Willy for a cousin?" the other girl said.

Now Lucky knew who they were. They were the girls Willy liked. He knew one was Erin and one was Celeste. He just wasn't sure which was which.

"What did you do to yourself?" the shorter one asked.

"I think I got Sasquatched."

"Oooh, that's bad," the blonde one, the taller one, said, and both girls giggled.

"So are you going to live here now, or what? Willy says you might move again."

"I don't know yet." Lucky was shading his eyes still, looking up toward the sun—and the faces.

And then one of them plunked herself down—just dropped, cross-legged onto the grass. And the other one did the same. The shorter one, with light brown hair, said, "You don't know us, do you?"

"I saw you both at church."

"You probably thought we were both pretty cute, didn't you?" Lucky was caught off guard. The truth was, she *was* cute. They both were. Lucky *had* thought that when he had seen them at church.

Lucky smiled, letting his bloody lip show. That didn't really matter. He had left his heart in Maui. He had nothing to lose here. "Actually," he said, "I remember thinking, 'What intelligent-looking girls. They must both be geniuses or something.'"

"Yeah. We're smart too. That's true."

This was from the shorter one again. She had pretty green eyes—sort of gray green—and a perfect face. Her skin was perfect, as was her cute little nose. Even the curve of her cheek bones and her sly smile were perfect. Lucky couldn't think of a way to improve anything.

But he glanced at the other one, with the blonde hair. She was blushing, big-time—and boy oh boy, did she look cute. "Quit it, Erin," she said.

"So your name is Erin?" Lucky said.

"Yup."

"And you're Celeste. Right?"

"Hey, you do know us," Erin said. "I figured you did."

"Willy told me your names. He likes both of you."

"I know," Erin said. "But we're not interested in him. We're breaking his heart. We like to do that."

Celeste laughed at that. And Lucky took another good look at her. He thought she might grow up to be a model someday—with those long, slender legs and long, blonde hair. She also had freckles across her nose, and one tooth that was just a little crooked. Somehow that made her look real. Lucky even liked the way she blushed.

"Celeste," Lucky said. "That's a good name. It sounds sort of . . . celestial . . . or something."

The redness in Celeste's cheeks had lightened a little, but now it came flooding back.

"So do you like her better than me?" Erin asked. Lucky would have hated to answer that honestly. Erin was such a knock-out. He even liked her style.

"No. I wouldn't say that."

"Would you say we're the two cutest girls you've ever seen?"

Erin didn't giggle, didn't blush. In fact, she was flirting with those green eyes the whole time.

Lucky figured he was blushing about as much as Celeste. But he answered honestly, "I'm not sure I could say that. I just came here from Maui. And I met a girl named Kaahu over there. She was *something!*"

"So are you in love with her?"

Lucky shrugged. "We're just friends, I guess."

Celeste finally spoke up. "Oooh, you can see it in his eyes, Erin. He *loves* her. We don't have a chance."

"You're right. Let's go." Erin started to get up.

"Don't give me that," Lucky said, surprising himself. "You two are the ones who have all the guys after you. You don't care about a dumb-looking guy like me."

"We don't care if you're dumb-looking. We want *all* boys to be after us. The more the better. Huh, Celeste?"

"Not if they're *really* dumb-looking."

"Well, yeah. Lucky's kind of cute." Erin was standing up now. "I guess we know when we're not wanted though."

"Yeah. We know when a guy is already in love with another girl—and we don't have a chance." Celeste got up too.

Maybe she wasn't so shy after all, Lucky thought—except that she was still blushing.

The two of them walked away, laughing and glancing back. Lucky didn't know what to think of them. Were they flirting just to give him a hard time—even making fun of him—or did they really sort of like him? He had no idea. But for some reason, he was suddenly more concerned about the way his lip looked. And his braces. And his glasses.

He really didn't need this.

Chapter 4

Lucky decided not to wait for Willy after all. He wanted to get some ice on his lip before the swelling worsened. The soccer fields were right by his school, so he had to walk only about four blocks.

When he got to Grandma's house, he was happy to find that Grandma wasn't home. She would have fussed too much. Lucky took a shower and dressed, and then he got a wash cloth and some ice and slipped out to the RV. He did his homework at the "kitchen" table while he held the ice to his lip. He liked being here, where he usually studied when he and his dad traveled. He felt at home.

In fact, Lucky was still in the RV when his dad got home from work. Lucky had left the door open to let some fresh air in, and Dad must have noticed it. He stepped in and said, "Hi, Lucky." Then he came inside.

For a moment he just looked around, as though he,

too, liked the feel of being back home. After a moment he walked over and sat down on the couch, which was also Lucky's bed when the two traveled. He finally seemed to notice the ice pack Lucky was holding. "What did you do to yourself?" he asked.

"I got run over—by a Sasquatch."

"What?"

"A soccer player. A great big guy. He stepped on me on his way to the goal."

Dad tried not to laugh, which meant he laughed only about twice as loud as most people do. "So did you guys lose again?"

"I'm not sure. I left early. But since we were behind nine to nothing, I have a feeling we probably did."

"The mighty Weasels," Dad said, and this time he bumped his laugh up a couple more points on the Richter scale.

But Lucky couldn't see much laughter in Dad's eyes, and Dad quieted more quickly than usual. Then he leaned forward and put his elbows on his knees. He was big enough to fill the room, it seemed. "Lucky, I've been thinking things over. It seems to me we ought to stay here in Provo permanently. Maybe we ought to start looking for a house to rent, or even to buy."

"Could we find something in this neighborhood?"

"Is this where you want to be?"

"Yeah. If possible. I'd like to have some long-term friends. And I know some kids around here now."

Dad nodded. "See. You want to put some roots down a little too, don't you?"

"Not necessarily. If you want to travel some more, that's okay with me. I'm just saying that if we stay in Provo, we might as well stay somewhere around here."

"I have no idea whether any houses are for sale in this neighborhood. I've noticed a couple of lots, though. Maybe we could buy a lot and hire someone to build us a house."

"In this ward?"

"Well, I don't know. That might be tough. Wards don't cover much territory around here. Do you really like this ward?"

Lucky actually didn't know whether he did or not, but he was experiencing some reactions he didn't quite understand. "Yeah, I guess. At least I know some of the kids."

Dad suddenly laughed again. Lucky thought he heard the metal on the side of the RV creak just a little from the blast. "I'll bet you've found yourself another girlfriend. That's what's up, isn't it? Lucky, you are such a ladies' man."

"Lay off, Dad. I haven't found a girlfriend." He thought of saying, "I've found two." But he knew better than to give information like that to his dad.

Still, the thought was very interesting—even confusing. Hadn't Lucky thought up till yesterday that there would never be another girl in the universe as perfect as Kaahu? How could he be thinking about *two* other girls already?

"You don't have to find girls, Lucky. They find you. You emit vibrations, and the girls just sort of home in on them. I don't know how you'll ever choose a wife. You have a girlfriend in every town in America, and now you're going to start collecting them around here."

"No, Dad. You've got it all wrong. Today a couple of girls told me I was *dumb*-looking. That's what girls think of me."

"Why? Because of your lip?"

"No. I'm dumb-looking without it. You might as well admit it."

"So what are you telling me? Were these girls being cruel and hateful?"

"No."

"Why did they say something like that then?"

"I don't know. I guess they were joking around or teasing, or something."

"Or were they flirting?"

"Not really."

"Hey. Come on. Tell the truth."

"I don't know. Maybe some."

"See. There you go. You've found yourself some

more female admirers. What a guy!" He slammed his
fist on his knee for emphasis.

But Dad didn't smile for long. Lucky had the feeling that he was only going through the motions, trying
to pretend that everything was normal between the two
of them.

After a few seconds Dad stood up. "Well, I'll let
you do your homework. But let's start looking around
for a house—or think about building one. I think it
would be better if you lived in the same place all
through junior high and high school."

He stepped toward the door.

"Dad?"

"Yeah?" His father turned around.

"I think you should still keep going out with Sister
Wakefield. Maybe that would be best for you." Lucky
couldn't really feel any conviction about that, but he
felt he should say it.

Dad just looked at Lucky for a time. "Well," he
finally said, "I'll see her once in a while."

"Dad, do you love her?"

Dad looked away. "I . . . guess so. We don't know
each other all that well yet."

"How can you tell when you love someone?"

"I don't know, Lucky. It's not as simple as it sounds
in the movies. I do know I like to be with her, and I
miss her when I can't—or don't—spend time with her."

"Would you be spending more time with her if it weren't for Tyler and me?"

"Yeah. I'm sure I would. It's more Tyler than you, though."

"Mom always said you should find someone else."

"I know. I didn't think I'd ever be ready for that. But when I met Carol, I started to think that I could."

His dad turned back to look at Lucky, but neither could look the other in the eye for long. Still, Lucky had to ask. "Can you love two people, one as much as the other?"

"I'm not sure, Lucky." He seemed to know what the question meant, however. "So far, I don't feel the same way about Carol that I did about your mom. But maybe I could, in time."

Lucky thought about Kaahu, and about Erin, and about Celeste. Strange. He considered telling his dad about the three of them and then asking what it all meant. But he decided he'd get teased too much, so he let it drop. He did think maybe he understood his dad a little better now.

Dad hadn't been gone long when Willy showed up. He was excited. "You should have stayed," he said as he leaped into the RV. "We did it!"

Lucky was astounded. "You *won?*"

Willy's wild arms suddenly dropped to his sides. "No. But we scored. And I sort of got an 'assist.'"

"What do you mean, 'sort of'?"

Willy grinned. He had obviously been home because he had changed out of his soccer uniform and had on an old pair of cut-off jeans and a T-shirt big enough for Crump, the Sasquatch. It hung almost to his knees. "The ball hit me in the back of the head and bounced right over to Spencer. He shot it into the net. Wouldn't you call that an assist?"

Lucky laughed. It sounded like a Weasel score all right. "So what was the final score?"

"I don't know. I didn't keep track. Fourteen to one or something like that. Hey, let's get out of here. It's too nice a day to hang around inside. How's your lip anyway?" He walked over and took a closer look.

"It's okay," Lucky said, "but I have to finish my homework."

"Finish it later. That lip needs fresh air."

"Yeah, right."

"Hey, I'm serious. Fresh air is the best cure for anything. I can have like a headache, or the flu, or almost anything, and I go outside and poof! I'm okay."

"I don't think it works on a swollen lip."

"Well, give it a shot. What can it hurt?"

The next thing Lucky knew, he had put away his homework and his ice pack, and he was walking down the street with Willy. It didn't take long, either, to see where Willy was heading. Right past Erin's house.

Lucky was pretty sure it was no accident that Erin and Celeste were sitting on the front lawn. Willy must have known that before he headed this way.

Lucky found his hand rising to his mouth, but he knew he couldn't hold it there all the time. He would just have to look dumb. Even dumber than usual.

"Hey, girls, what's happening?" Willy shouted, trying to act surprised at seeing them.

"We're waiting for guys to come by and gawk at us," Erin said. "Because we're so beautiful."

Willy walked onto the lawn, sat down in front of Erin, and stared at her. "I gotta admit," he said after a time, "you're not bad. Just not good enough for me and Lucky."

"Really?" Erin asked in mock seriousness. "What does it take to be good enough for guys like you?"

"We don't know," Willy said with the same serious tone. "So far, we haven't found anyone who's up to our standards."

"Lucky has," Celeste said. "He found the perfect girl in Hawaii. Oahu—or something like that."

"Kaahu," Lucky told her.

"So you admit it?"

Lucky rolled his eyes. His hand rose, as if by itself, to cover his mouth again.

"How's your lip?" Celeste asked.

"Okay. It'll just take a few days to heal up."

"You should put some ice on it."

"I did."

"Fresh air is the best thing." Willy was still staring at Erin.

Erin looked up at Lucky. "Is your dad going to marry Tyler's mom?"

"No way. That's all over," Willy said before Lucky could answer.

"Really?"

Willy nodded.

"Yup. Tyler was being a jerk about it. And he got his way. I wanted Uncle Ron to marry Sister Wakefield so I could hang out over there. Kristin's good enough looking even for me."

Lucky expected all the kidding to start again, but Erin was still looking at Lucky. "Did you want your dad to marry Sister Wakefield?"

"I don't know. It's not my decision."

Willy stepped in again. "Would you want to be Tyler's *brother?* That's about the worst thing that could happen to a person."

"Maybe not. A person could have *you* for a brother. That'd be worse."

"No way. I'm a good brother. The only thing you girls notice about me is that I'm so good-looking. But I have lots of other excellent qualities."

Erin began making gagging sounds. But Celeste

said to Lucky seriously, "Tyler's not so bad. He was always sort of nice until—you know—all that stuff happened in their family."

"Hey, lots of people get divorces," Willy said. "Kristin didn't change. Tyler's the only one who fell apart."

"How does he treat you, Lucky?" Celeste asked.

"Rotten!" Willy answered.

Lucky wasn't quite so harsh. "Pretty bad. When my dad and I were here before, we started to be friends—a little. But now he won't even talk to me."

"He's such a geek," Willy mumbled. And Erin nodded.

Celeste shook her head. "If my parents got divorced, I probably wouldn't want them to get married to other people. Especially if I had to have a new mom, or a new dad."

"Hey," Willy said, "Lucky doesn't want a new mom either. But he doesn't act like a jerk about it."

Lucky wasn't completely sure about that.

"Was it hard for you when your mom died, Lucky?" Celeste asked.

The question surprised Lucky. In fact the whole conversation was surprising. He hardly knew these girls. "Sure," he mumbled.

"But you got over it," she said. "I'll bet Tyler gets over his dad leaving. It's just going to take some time."

"Some things you don't get over," Lucky said. "You just learn to live with them."

Everyone was looking at Lucky. Even Willy had turned around.

"Lucky, you're nice," Erin said. "I didn't know that." She hesitated and then added, "How could you be cousins with Willy—that's what I'd like to know?"

Lucky shrugged, and Willy protested. Lucky noticed that Celeste was still watching him. He covered his mouth again.

Chapter 5

*T*he next morning at school, Erin and Celeste—especially Erin—continued to tease Lucky every chance they got. They had both remembered the name Kaahu, and they whispered it to him as they walked past him in the hallway. And in the cafeteria after lunch, they stopped Lucky and asked whether his broken heart would ever heal.

Willy was with Lucky, of course, and he told the girls, "Get a life, will you? Why do you keep bugging Lucky about some girl you've never met?"

"We feel sorry for him," Erin said. "His heart is broken. We want to help him forget, but we're not ravishingly beautiful like Ka-aaaa-huuuu."

"Admit the truth," Willy said. "You're both nuts over me."

"We would be nuts, all right, if we were."

"Hey, I know what you're up to. You're paying all

this attention to Lucky to make me jealous. But anyone can see I'm the good-looking one around here." Willy struck a muscle-man pose, with his arms bowed out in front and his shoulders hunched forward. "Check those pecs!" he grunted.

Both girls laughed. Then Celeste said, "Willy, you ought to try being nice, just once. Like Lucky. Maybe that's what girls like."

"Hey, I'm the nicest guy I know," Willy said, and he looked at Lucky as though expecting his agreement. The girls were already walking away. "I think I'm *very* nice," Willy said to their backs.

Celeste turned and called back to Lucky, "I hope your poor lip gets better fast."

"Hey, what's the big interest in Lucky's lips all of a sudden?" Willy called to her. The girls kept going.

"You're way too nice, Willy," Lucky said. "I think that's your problem."

"Now that's something I can agree with." Willy made one of those strange chopping motions that seemed to come from nowhere. Then he started to walk. Lucky followed, not exactly sure where they were going.

Willy headed outside toward the playground. They still had about ten minutes before the bell was going to ring. "So what's the deal, Lucky?" Willy asked as they got outside. "Your dad said you lost your mind over that Kow-huey girl over in Hawaii."

"Kaahu."

"So what's going on? Are you throwing her over already—for Celeste?"

"What are you talking about? I haven't said anything about Celeste."

"I've watched how you check her out all the time. Erin's cuter, if you ask me."

"Yeah, well, I've seen you looking at *her.* Plenty."

"What's wrong with that?"

"So do you really like her or something?"

"Yup. But she doesn't exactly feel the same way about me."

"That's because of the way you act around her."

"It ain't no act, Lucky. It's just me. They gotta love me for who I am." Willy began to strut as he walked. "So which one do you think is the cutest?"

"I think they're both pretty cute."

"Oh, brother, Lucky. You're a mess."

"What're you talking about? You said they were both your girlfriends."

"I know. But I was lying. They don't like me. They're not kidding about that part."

"That's just their way of flirting with you."

Willy stopped and looked at Lucky. "No way. Not a chance. Never, ever. No, never. Uh-uh." Willy had his baseball cap on, backwards, so at least his hair was out of his eyes. He looked almost serious that way.

"I'm not so sure about that."

"Well, you're wrong. I speak with a straight tongue." Willy stuck his tongue straight out to prove it.

"You just told me you were lying before."

"See. That proves it. I told you the truth about lying. So now I'll tell you the truth about truth. Girls don't like me."

Lucky was surprised. Up to this point, Lucky had thought that Willy was just kidding around, as always. But he seemed serious now.

"How would you like to have my face?" Lucky said. "I look like a beaver with braces. I'm the funniest-looking guy around."

"Yeah, I know. So how come that girl in Hawaii didn't care about that?"

"Maybe she did. She'll find a real boyfriend some-day—one who looks a lot better."

"If she does, she's stupid," Willy said. Lucky was surprised again—Willy was being . . . nice.

Willy finally turned and looked out toward the play-ground, as though he were going to size up what was going on out there. But Lucky knew he was embar-rassed.

Just then a voice came from behind the boys. "Look. It must be a family reunion. The Doofus cousins are together again."

Tyler Wakefield.

Lucky didn't even turn around. He started to walk away. But Willy said, "Tyler, shut your mouth. All right?"

Lucky didn't want this.

Lucky and Tyler had avoided each other most of the time, and Lucky figured that was best. This time Tyler had some of his buddies with him. Lucky had learned their names—Blake and Ben and Warren—but that's all he knew about them except that they all seemed to have attitudes like Tyler's. Tyler got a lot more mouthy when he was with these guys.

"I heard what you guys have been saying about me," Tyler said. "You don't have the guts to say it to my face."

"To tell you the truth, Tyler," Willy said, "the only thing I can remember saying about you is that you're a jerk. Oh, and I think I said you were a geek. But you already know that—so what's the big problem?"

"I'll fight you any time you want to fight," Tyler said.

The statement struck Lucky as illogical, but the fact that Tyler was talking to Lucky and not to Willy was the bigger surprise.

"Have a nice day, Tyler," Lucky said sarcastically,

and he forced a big smile—which pulled his lip too hard, and hurt.

"Thanks, Lucky. I'm having very good days now that my mom told your dad to shove off."

Suddenly Lucky's sympathy was gone. The guy really was a jerk. Lucky still wasn't going to get into it with him, though.

"Tyler, just shut your mouth," Willy said. "That's not what happened and you know it."

Tyler was still looking at Lucky. "You two aren't moving in on us, Lucky. Your dad better not ever come near my mom again."

Willy stepped forward and pointed a finger in Tyler's face. "Hey, I'll tell you what really happened. Your mom came after Uncle Ron right from the beginning. I know. I was there when it happened. Grandma had it all set up. Uncle Ron didn't know one thing about it, and your mom came over all dressed up, and wearing lots of makeup and everything. And she was smiling and flirting and the whole business."

"You *liar!*" Tyler came at Willy with his fists doubled.

Lucky stepped in fast, however, and grabbed Tyler tight, pinning his arms to his sides. "Okay, that's enough," Lucky said.

Tyler fought free and stepped back. Lucky was expecting him to go after Willy again, and maybe that's why he didn't see the blow coming. Suddenly Tyler's fist was flying toward his eyes—his glasses. Lucky threw his head back to avoid the blow, but Tyler's knuckles caught him right in the mouth.

On the lip. The same lip.

Lucky spun away and grabbed his mouth, but he could already taste the blood. His braces had cut even deeper this time.

By then Willy was on Tyler. He grabbed him and threw him backward, and then was about to pounce. Lucky jumped back into the action. He grabbed Willy around the shoulders and pulled him away. "I told you guys that's enough," Lucky shouted.

"Yeah. You're afraid to fight me," Tyler said, but he was stepping backward. Lucky could see that he was actually afraid of something—probably not Lucky, but maybe afraid to fight. Maybe afraid of getting in trouble. Maybe afraid of what his mother would say about this.

So the fight ended, and the boys went back into the building. Lucky's lip was worse than ever. He stopped in the boys' room and got some paper towels, which he wet down. When he got back to class, he told his teacher, Mr. Carey, that he had bumped into a guy and got his sore lip bleeding again. That was at least half the truth.

Willy was astounded. "Why don't you tell on him? He had no reason to punch you like that."

"It's okay," Lucky said. He told Mr. Carey he wouldn't need to go to the nurse. Then he told himself that he was all right, that getting his face banged up was nothing new. He could take it.

By now, however, the word was spreading fast. The kids in the class all knew that Tyler had hit Lucky. Celeste came over to Lucky's desk before the bell rang. "Are you okay?" she asked.

"Yeah. Sure," Lucky said, trying to act as though it were no big deal.

Celeste actually seemed concerned. She wasn't teasing him. "It's that same lip, isn't it?"

"Yeah."

"You poor thing."

Lucky felt a certain lightness in his head—and it wasn't entirely from being punched. "I'm all right." He tried to sound manly and brave. "It doesn't hurt that bad."

"Let's see," she said.

Lucky pulled the paper towel away.

"Ooooh. It's bad, Lucky. You need ice . . . or something."

Lucky shrugged. "It's no big deal. I've been hurt worse." He hunched his shoulders forward a little—sort of the way Willy had done when he was trying to show off his muscles.

Celeste shook her head, as if to say, "You're so brave." Then she went back to her desk.

It was after school when Erin finally got a chance to inspect the lip. What she said surprised Lucky. "It was my fault."

"Your fault? Why?"

"Sometimes I talk too much. Maybe you never noticed that."

"Talk too much?" Lucky said. "You?" He was trying to show that he could still joke around, but his lip was swollen enough that speech was a little difficult.

"I was smarting off to Tyler this morning, and I told him what Willy said about him. I shouldn't have done that, I know, but mostly I just talk, and then I do my thinking afterwards."

"Mostly she doesn't think at all," Celeste said over Erin's shoulder.

"I know. That's true," Erin said. "That really is true. And I've got to change. I really do. I'm going to start tomorrow—or the next day. So where's Willy?"

"Soccer practice."

"I guess you can't go today."

"It doesn't matter much whether I go or not."

"Yeah, I could tell that. You're a pretty bad player, aren't you?"

"Erin, maybe you ought to start changing today," Celeste said, and she smiled at Lucky.

"Do you *really* think I need to change?" Erin asked Lucky, acting very surprised. "I just said that, but I didn't mean it."

Lucky shook his head. He tried not to laugh because laughing hurt. "So do you like Willy or something?" he asked Erin.

"Willy? Are you kidding? Why would you think that?"

"I don't know. You were just asking about him."

"When?"

"You asked me where he was."

"Oh. Well, that's because I love to be around him. He's weird and everything, but he's madly in love with me—and I just love it when guys are in love with me. You haven't fallen for me yet, have you, Lucky?"

"I guess not."

"I don't care if you love Celeste *and* me. I just don't like it when guys don't fall in love with me at all. It ruins my self-esteem."

"Well, maybe I can start tomorrow—or the next day."

"Okay. But put some ice on that lip. You look awful with it sticking out like that. You don't have to be like a movie star or anything, but it's better if you don't look really gross."

"Okay. I'll see what I can do about it."

"If it doesn't get better by tomorrow, just keep your crush on Celeste for a while and hold off on me. Okay?"

"Erin, just be quiet for once," Celeste said.

That was pretty good advice, Lucky thought.

Chapter 6

Lucky usually didn't hide things from his dad. This time, though, he really didn't want a big deal made out of this problem with Tyler. If Lucky said something to Dad, and Dad said something to Sister Wakefield, that would only get Tyler in trouble, and that would make things worse. Lucky just wanted things to calm down.

So he told his dad he had bumped into someone, the same as he had told Mr. Carey. Grandma fussed a little, but there wasn't a single thing she could do. She considered putting a plastic bandage on the inside of his lip, but Lucky convinced her that it wouldn't work.

When Lucky went to bed that night, he figured he had at least avoided making the mess any bigger. But he was still worried. If his dad continued to see Sister Wakefield with the hope that Tyler would get used to the idea, things would probably get much worse before they ever got better. Lucky really didn't want to deal with Tyler. True, Lucky didn't want the guy for a brother, but he didn't want to make Dad miserable either. There was no way to win.

So Lucky was troubled as he drifted off to sleep. He was still asleep—somewhere in the middle of the night—when he heard a noise. It was like a huge truck, or maybe a train. And someone was shaking Lucky's bed.

"Don't," Lucky said. Dad or Grandma, or someone, was rocking his bed back and forth, making it flop around like a hammock. And it was still way too early to get up.

Suddenly Lucky was awake. He was hearing crashing noises. Things were falling. Glass was breaking. And still his bed was rolling, rolling. Lucky thought something had hit the house—the truck he had heard, or maybe a tree had fallen.

And then he knew.

"Earthquake!" he yelled, although he didn't know who could hear him.

Lucky had felt one in California, but it had been nothing like this. The motion, the rolling, just kept going and going. Lucky could hear the house creaking and twisting, and he thought the place couldn't hold together much longer. Then something heavy dropped to the floor, and a whole series of thuds followed.

Lucky wanted to run outside, get out of the house.

But he was too frightened to run into the blackness. Somewhere he had heard that he should get into a doorway for protection, and he even told himself to do it. But the rolling and rattling wouldn't stop, and he felt pinned to the bed. Something else was crashing too—maybe out in the kitchen. Lucky couldn't make himself move.

Then it stopped.

Lucky sat still, listening and waiting, when he heard his dad's voice. "Lucky, are you all right?"

"Yeah."

"Okay. Stay put." And then, after a pause: "The lights are out. Just stay where you are. I'll get a flashlight."

By then Grandpa was shouting, "Ron? Lucky? Are you okay?"

"Yes. We're okay," Dad shouted back. "Don't walk around with your shoes off. There's glass on the floor. Where are your flashlights?"

"There's one in the hall closet. But the batteries are pretty well shot."

"I have a big one in the RV. Stay where you are. I'm getting dressed. I'll go get it."

Grandma was out there in the dark somewhere, too. "Ron, don't we need to turn the gas off?"

"Not necessarily. Let me get that flashlight, and then I'll check things out. Don't try to walk around until we have some light—and get your shoes on. We're okay. Just stay calm."

Lucky was telling himself the same thing. Everything was okay. It was over. Some things had broken in the house, but no one was hurt. And yet he was trembling all over. He grasped his arms tight around his chest, but the panic inside him kept getting worse, not better. He had the terrible feeling that the house was going to cave in even though the rolling had stopped. If only it weren't so dark.

Dad came back from the RV in a couple of minutes. He yelled, "Everyone just stay where you are. I'm going downstairs to check for gas leaks—or water."

"We have our water heater strapped to the wall," Grandpa yelled back to him.

"Good," Dad said.

Lucky heard him thump down the stairs. He hoped there weren't any problems. He still wanted to run outside before the house fell in—or blew up.

In a few minutes Dad came upstairs. He had a bright flashlight, and that helped Lucky more than anything. Dad came in and checked Lucky's bedroom floor to be certain there was no glass. He hugged Lucky, which calmed Lucky even more, and then he waited until Lucky hurried and dressed.

Grandpa found a dim little light, and the two of them checked the house upstairs. Lucky followed.

Things could have been worse. Falling books had made the thudding noises, and a mirror in the living room had fallen and shattered—along with a lot of Grandma's ceramic pieces. Some dishes in a hutch, in the dining room, had hit the glass door and cracked it, but the dishes hadn't fallen out. The kitchen was the biggest mess, with pots and pans and canned goods on the floor, but nothing much was broken.

Lucky followed his Dad, wanting to be close but not wanting to admit it. Dad turned on a water faucet in the kitchen. "There's darn little pressure here," he told Grandpa. "A water main must be broken somewhere in the neighborhood. There's no leak in the house anywhere that I could see. And I couldn't smell gas anywhere. So we don't need to turn anything off."

Grandma had remained surprisingly quiet through all this. Dad finally said, "Sorry about all those figurines and things. A lot of them are broken."

But Grandma said, "I don't care a hoot about any of that. I'm worried about Carol. She and those girls must be terrified over there. We're okay here. Why don't you go check on her? And Sister Fenton down the street. She's all alone."

"Does your ward have any sort of emergency plan?" Dad asked.

"Not that I know of," Grandpa said. "Maybe home

teachers should check on people. I think someone said something like that in priesthood meeting one time."

"Okay, listen," Dad said. "Do you have any water stored?"

"No. We have a couple of those seventy-two-hour kit things. But I've never looked at what's in them."

"Okay. We've got plenty of food around here. I've also got the propane stove in the RV. Fill up some containers with water while you still have some pressure. We can also use the water in the water heater and in the toilet tanks. I'm going to head over to Carol's, and then I'll check with the bishop and see what kind of a plan is in place."

Lucky was glad his dad knew what to do. It was still dark outside. He wished the sun would come up. "What time is it?" he asked.

"It's almost three o'clock," Dad said. "We're not going to have any light for quite a while." He paused and thought. "We'll probably have some aftershocks, and most people don't like to ride those out inside their homes. Mom, why don't you collect some water and go out to the RV. Lucky, you get a jacket. It's pretty cool out. Then come with me. Dad, you could check on Sister Fenton."

Lucky was already feeling his way down the dark hallway, heading to his bedroom to get his jacket. Since

Grandma had mentioned the Wakefields, Lucky had begun to think how frightened they all must be.

Dad followed Lucky, shining the light down the hall. Lucky was still shaking. He kept saying to himself that it wasn't too bad—just a few things broken—but his body didn't want to believe it.

Lucky found his jacket, and he and his dad made their way to the front door. Dad tugged, and it opened with a grating sound. "This door is out of line a little," Dad told his parents. "You might want to check some of the other outside doors. That'll give you an idea of whether the house took any structural damage."

With that, the Ladds headed out. Dad went to the RV first and took out a big first-aid box. Then he took off on a fast walk, making Lucky trot to keep up. Dad flashed his light toward the first house they passed by. Inside, Lucky could see flashlights and candles. "I hope these people know what they're doing," Dad said. "We could be completely on our own for a few days— maybe longer."

"Should we stop and tell them what to do?"

"We'll talk to the bishop. We'll help however we can. But I've just got to check on Carol first."

For the first time, Lucky heard worry in his Dad's voice. Lucky felt his own panic well up again. Maybe there were people really badly hurt. Maybe houses would explode, or catch on fire. Maybe this whole thing wasn't over yet.

Along the street they found that most people had already gone outside where they felt more safe. Evidently they had grabbed blankets or coats on the way out. Dad gave them each some advice, but people seemed too stunned to pay much attention.

When Lucky and his dad got to the Wakefields' house, Dad pounded hard on the front door. He even tried to open it, but it was locked. Inside, Lucky could see some sort of light, back in the kitchen maybe. Then the light moved toward the door, and Lucky knew it was a flashlight.

Carol pulled the door open, and Lucky caught a glance of her face. He saw tears on her cheeks. "Oh, Ron, thank you," she said. "I'm so scared."

And then Dad was holding her in his arms. She was wearing a long nightgown, and there she was clinging to Lucky's dad, and Lucky didn't mind—didn't even give it much thought.

Kristin was there, behind, in the dark. "What are we supposed to do?" she said. And Lucky heard a little sob. "Tyler said we have to turn the gas off. He's outside somewhere trying to figure out how to do it."

Dad let go of Carol. "Do you all have your shoes on?" Dad asked.

"We do now," Carol said. "But Heather cut her foot really bad. She's in the kitchen."

"Okay. We'll take care of that," Dad said. "Have you smelled any gas?"

"No."

"Any water running?"

"I don't think so."

"All right. Tyler shouldn't turn the gas off unless there's a leak. It could be several days before the gas company could get out here to turn it back on. Lucky, you go out and stop him, and I'll check the water heater and the furnace."

"He's out in back," Kristin said, and now she was crying harder.

"Run around the house, Lucky," Carol said. "Hurry."

"Hey, it's okay if he turned it off," Dad said, putting an arm around Kristin. "It won't hurt anything. It's just better if we can keep it on. See if you can catch him in time, Lucky."

Lucky took off. He ran around the house and then had a little trouble getting the gate to the fence open. Finally he ran into the backyard. "Tyler, wait," he yelled. "Don't turn it off." Lucky could see a light from a flashlight at the far end of the house. He ran toward it, across the back lawn.

"Don't turn it off," he yelled. Suddenly the light was shining in his eyes. "Dad said not to."

Tyler's voice shot back like a poisoned arrow. "I *have* to turn it off. That's what we're supposed to do."

Lucky slowed down as he approached. He shaded his eyes from the light. "Did you get it turned off already?"

The flashlight turned back toward the meter. "No. But I'm going to. We learned about this stuff in Scouts."

"Dad said if there's no leak, it's better not to turn it off. He's down checking for leaks right now."

Tyler was looking at the meter. Lucky could see his face, only dimly. He seemed not to know what to do. He was still looking, as though he were searching for the shut-off valve. "You and your dad can go," he mumbled. "We don't need you here. I'll take care of everything."

Lucky could see that Tyler had a wrench in his hand. But it was the wrong kind. He needed some sort of slotted tool, or even some pliers. Lucky knelt down next to him. "Look, Tyler, this looks like the shut-off thing. But you can't turn it with that kind of wrench. Let's go find some pliers, and then if Dad yells to shut it off, we can do it."

But Tyler tried to hook the wrench over the head of the valve and make it work somehow.

"Tyler, listen! My dad knows all about this stuff. We've been in all kinds of situations like this. He *knows*."

Tyler was still trying to lodge the wrench against the valve head.

"Don't, Tyler! Really!" Lucky grabbed at Tyler's hand. At the same moment Tyler's arm lashed out. The wrench and the back of Tyler's fist slammed into Lucky's chest.

Lucky was knocked back for a moment, but he came back hard. He tackled Tyler and knocked him to the ground. Then Lucky felt the thud of the flashlight over the top of his head.

Lucky grasped Tyler's arm and stopped him from swinging again. The two rolled over on the grass. Lucky was trying to get hold of the wrench when he heard his dad. "Hey, boys, don't turn it off."

Lucky rolled off Tyler, and Tyler scrambled up. He still had the flashlight in his hand. He pointed it at Dad. "Leave us alone!" he screamed. But he was already crying, sobs breaking from his throat, which he was trying to stop. "Leave us alone. We're *supposed* to turn it off."

Dad walked over close, and Lucky was afraid that Tyler might take a swing at him. He didn't, and Dad stepped next to him and slid his arm around his shoulder. "I'm glad you were trying to manage things here," he said. "You acted like a man. But I'm glad you didn't get it shut off."

Tyler didn't say anything. He just cried. Then Dad pulled him a little tighter and said, "Everything's okay. Your sister cut her foot, and we need to get that taken care of. But your house isn't hurt—just a few things broken inside. There's nothing to be afraid of now."

Lucky couldn't believe what he was seeing. Tyler wasn't moving back. He was clinging to Lucky's dad, crying, with his head against his chest. "That's what they told us at Scouts," he said, trying desperately to stop crying.

"I know. Lots of people say that. And it is the safest thing to do. But everything is okay, and we might as well have the heat, once the electricity comes back on."

Tyler finally stepped away. Lucky saw him nod. "Okay," he said. "We were scared the house might blow up. That's all."

Lucky understood what Tyler must have been feeling. Lucky knew how frightened he had been when the earthquake had hit. What if his dad hadn't been there?

"You did the right thing," Dad said, and he patted Tyler on the shoulder. "You were looking out for your family." Dad pulled him close again, hugged him, and patted him on the back. And Tyler let him do it.

When Dad walked back into the house, Tyler followed, although he hung back, as though he were now embarrassed.

Dad got out his first-aid kit and worked on Heather's foot. She cried and clung to her mother while Dad cleaned the wound. "It's pretty deep, but it's in the pad of her foot," Dad said. "I don't think she cut any tendons or anything like that. It'll just be sore for a while."

"All my stuff fell on the floor," Heather said, sobbing. "It was crashing down in the dark, and falling and falling and falling. I couldn't see anything. I didn't know what to do. So I ran."

She kept talking on and on and kept crying while everyone watched in the dim light as Kristin held the flashlight. Molly was clinging to her mother, crying too.

Lucky stepped over next to Tyler. "I was so scared," he told Tyler. "I thought the house was going to cave in on us."

Tyler nodded. "Yeah. Me too," he said.

Chapter 7

When Lucky and his dad left the Wakefields, they hurried to the bishop's house. As they walked, Lucky could hear sirens, and he could see a glow in the sky that seemed a couple of blocks away. Dad said a house was probably on fire.

When Lucky and his dad got to Bishop Hess's, a little group of men were standing on the front lawn, surrounding the bishop. Lucky heard one of the men say, "What about Sister Lancaster? Someone better go over and check on her. I'll do that if you want." The man turned to go.

Another man said, "I saw Brother Miller when I was walking over here. He said he was checking on the widows."

Someone else said, "Brother Bennion will check on Sister Lancaster. He always—"

And then the bishop's voice boomed over the others, "*Wait a minute!* Don't everyone talk at once. I told Brother Kent to check on the widows. He's the high priest group leader. That's his responsibility. We've got to get this thing organized."

Dad stepped up then and said, "Bishop, I've had a lot of experience with this sort of thing. Can I help you?"

Lucky saw Bishop Hess's face caught in the glow of a flashlight. He had always seemed confident and relaxed to Lucky, but he looked worried now. "Brother Ladd," he said, "I hate to say it, but we're not ready for this. I'm not sure what to do."

"Do you have any sort of emergency plan?"

"Not really. President Hadley asked us to get one worked out, but we haven't gotten very far on it."

"The first thing is to account for all the people," Dad said, "and assess the damage to the houses."

"That's what we were trying to do. But people are running all over the place. I don't know how to get control of things. Someone just came over and said that we've got some houses that have caved in, over along the edge of the hill."

"Are the people out?"

"I don't know. We need to get someone down there to work on that."

"I'd suggest you put some teams together and start checking every house. They can see if anyone's hurt, give first aid, check on gas and water—and account for all the people, as much as possible."

"Yeah, okay. That's sort of what we've been doing. But I can't get people to hold still long enough to take assignments. We're not sure who's gone where—and we don't have any way to get reports back."

"The people who've gone out so far—do they have first-aid kits with them?"

"Uh . . . I'm not sure. I think . . . someone had one, or at least said he would get one. Who was that?" The bishop looked around, but no one seemed to know.

"If I were you," Brother Ladd said, "I'd get out a ward map and assign sections to the men who are here right now. Have them account for all the people and bring back their reports. Don't worry about whether anyone has been through that area before. Get your own reports. And as more people show up here, keep assigning sections and getting reports until everyone is accounted for."

"All right. That sounds good. I think we'd better get down to those caved-in houses first. That sounds the worst."

"I'll take some men and head over there," Dad said. "I've got a good first-aid kit. Does anyone else here have one?"

"I think we have one over at the church," the bishop

said. "Or maybe the Scoutmaster has it. I'm not sure. People in the ward must have some."

"Are there any doctors in the ward?"

"No. We've got some nurses though."

"Okay. If you get reports of injuries, I'd try to get those nurses—and first-aid materials—to the people who are hurt. Calling 911 will be pointless. Even if the lines aren't down, the system will be jammed, and there's no way the ambulances in town can handle all this. If people are hurt, it may be up to us to keep them alive. And we could be talking days, not just hours."

"Do you think we ought to set up a shelter in the church—for those who can't get back into their homes?"

"Is there any damage to the church?"

"Someone said it looked okay. We haven't been inside yet."

"Okay. Here are a couple of things to think about: The city just might be evacuating people out of the river bottoms—on the chance that the dam could break. They'll have to head onto the hill. Plus, you have most people in the ward standing around outside. So the church might be a resource at some point. But remember, it's a big, dark building, and with the water pressure gone, the toilets won't be working. Most people absolutely refuse to go inside for a while anyway."

"Where are we going to put people then?"

"People would usually rather camp out in their yards than go back in. I'd start finding out if your members have enough camping equipment. Some of the people might not be prepared to stay out of their houses for a few days."

Bishop Hess was nodding again, his glasses reflecting the light from the flashlights around him. "Okay. At least it will be light before long. We'll have all day to get that worked out. Let's get some crews going now and see whether we have injuries. You'd better get over to the edge of the hill. We've got some older people in those homes. I just pray they're all right. Someone said the Hamptons' house is almost flattened."

"Okay. Someone might have them out by now. But I'll check all the houses. And I'll get a report back to you. If you can get hold of one of the nurses, I think I'd send her over there. We're bound to have some injuries."

The bishop asked two other men to go with Dad, and the three headed away, with Lucky following. Dad didn't get far before he shouted back, "Bishop, does anyone have a transistor radio? We need to know what's going on."

"We have one. But the batteries are about shot. My wife was looking for some more batteries."

"Okay. I have one in my RV. You might check with my dad."

The bishop was nodding. "Okay. Thanks," he said. "I'm glad you're here."

Dad was off again at a fast walk, taking those huge strides of his. The two men with him had to work hard to keep up, and Lucky had to jog. Dad seemed to know one of the men. "Reed, you're a builder, aren't you?" Dad asked him.

He was a sturdy-looking man. Lucky had seen earlier, in the light from the flashlights, that he was maybe Dad's age. "Yeah, I am."

"Good. We may need to brace some places up."

"Oh, sure. I can do that."

The other man said, "I'm a history professor. I can tell the people that the Saints had it tougher back in Nauvoo."

Dad chuckled and put out his hand. "Ron Ladd," he said.

"Bill Dayley," the man replied. He looked rather frail alongside Dad and the other man, but he was smiling, and Lucky hadn't seen anyone else do that.

"I've seen some situations worse than this," Dad said. "But I'll tell you what worries me. If we've got some houses down with people inside, we may need to go in and get them out. Someone could bleed to death if we wait for help."

Lucky was still jogging to keep up. Suddenly he realized that someone was running along just behind him, pulling even. He glanced back and saw a figure a little bigger than himself.

"Hi," Lucky said.

"I came to help."

Lucky knew the voice. It was Tyler's. "Some houses are down," Lucky said. "We're going to see what we can do."

"I know," Tyler said. "The bishop told me. I've got my first-aid stuff."

Lucky knew this was more than just an offer to help. It was a peace offering.

Dad looked back, flashed a light across Tyler, and said, "Good. Have you got any big bandages?"

"Uh . . . not really. Just little ones and some gauze and stuff."

Lucky couldn't see what he was carrying, but he seemed to be holding it in one hand. It was nothing like Dad's big kit.

"That's all right. Anything you've got might come in handy."

"Do you know first aid?"

"I got my merit badge not too long ago. I think I remember some of it."

Tyler didn't sound very confident, but Dad said, "Good. That's what we need."

About then a man came running out of the dark.

"Are you guys coming to help?" he shouted, and he sounded anxious.

"Yeah, we are," Reed said.

"Oh, Brother Sneddon. I'm glad you're here. We've got a mess." The man had already turned around and was leading the way back in the darkness. "Hurry," he said. "We pulled Sister Steele out of her house, but she's hurt pretty bad. And her husband is banged up too. The Hamptons' house is right down on the ground. We can't even get inside."

Dad and the other men raced after him. As they rounded the corner, Lucky could see flashlights and people moving in front of the second house. A group seemed to be gathered together.

Lucky could see that someone—a woman—was lying on the grass in front of the house, and people were working on her.

Dad wasn't gentle. He pushed right into the circle and said, "What does she need? I've got a first-aid kit."

"Oh, thank goodness," a woman said. "I need bandages. Disinfectant. But I think she's got broken ribs too, and maybe internal injuries."

Lucky could see that Sister Steele's head was bleeding. She wasn't moving at all.

Reed said to Dad, "Julie's a nurse."

Julie looked up as the light caught her face. She had red hair, and in the half light she seemed pale. But her voice was strong. "We need to get her to the hospital if we can."

Dad said, "Can we stop the bleeding and then take her to the hospital ourselves—in a car, or in the back of a truck? I don't think we have much chance of getting an ambulance."

"We might have to," Julie said. "She shouldn't be moved that way. But if she's bleeding inside, we've got to get her to a hospital. She could die if we wait too long."

Lucky was leaning forward with his hands on his knees when he felt a little rolling motion under his feet. He stood up straight and felt a series of hard shakes run through his legs. They lasted only a few seconds, and then they were gone.

"Aftershock," someone said.

Someone yelled from down the street, "We've got to get into the Hamptons' house before it gives way on us."

Somewhere in the middle of all that, Lucky heard a muffled boom, quite far away. Someone said, "Something just blew up—somewhere to the south."

Lucky looked off the hill, in the distance, and for a moment he didn't see anything. Then he saw the glow of fire.

This new shake—new fire—brought all the fear

back. Maybe the quakes would keep coming. Maybe bigger ones. Maybe everything would cave in.

That's when Lucky heard Tyler, who was standing next to him, say, "I don't know where my dad is."

Lucky wasn't sure what to say. He waited a moment, then said, "Where does he live?"

"In Orem. In an apartment. It's on the bottom floor."

Lucky knew what he was fearing. "He'll be all right," Lucky said, not knowing what else to say. Lucky was standing close enough to Tyler that he could feel him quivering.

Dad had stood up now. "Does anyone know for sure that the Hamptons were home?"

"I'm sure they were," someone said. "They don't really go anywhere."

"Okay. Come on then. We've got to get them out of there," Dad said. Then he turned to Julie. "You keep this kit. If you think you need to take her to the hospital, get some of these men to help you."

Lucky was amazed at the way everyone listened to Dad. Most of them knew a little about him, but more than anything he sounded strong—someone who knew what to do.

Now he was moving down the street again, shining his light ahead of him. "Lucky, are you coming?"

"Yeah. I'm right behind you."

"Tyler, do you have your first-aid kit?"

"Yeah."

"Okay. Don't get near the house. But don't wander off either."

Both boys said, "All right."

At the Hamptons' house, Lucky could feel the panic in all the voices. Several men were standing together, and they all seemed to be talking at the same time. Dad stepped up to them. "I'm Ron Ladd. I think you know my parents."

"Sure we do. I'm Randy Davidson," one of them said. He was a young man, rather tall and slender. "We've got to get in there somehow. But we're not sure how we can do it. Everything is really unstable."

"We've got to be careful," Reed said. "This whole place looks like it could slide down the hill."

"Where was their bedroom?" Dad asked.

"In the back, over on the far side. They had a walk-out basement. Some of the hill gave way and slid right out from under the house. The whole back of the house has dropped into what used to be the basement. Come down here and look."

Dad walked around the house with the other men. Lucky could see a short man with a big mustache. Someone called him Brother Bennion. Lucky didn't know who the others were.

The men flashed their lights around, and Lucky

could see that the back of the house had given way and slid down the hill. The back end of the roof was almost to the ground.

Dad knelt down and tried to see under the roof. "Have you heard anything? Have you tried to call to them?"

"Yeah, we have," Brother Davidson said. "We're not getting any response at all. I'm afraid everything came right in on top of them."

"Well, we're going to have to get in there before it's too late for them," Dad said.

"Not if we have to take the chance of putting someone else's life in danger," Reed said.

Lucky felt a chill run all the way through him. He was afraid his dad would be willing to take that chance.

Chapter 8

*D*ad and Reed talked things over quickly.

"I guess we can cut a section of this roof away and get in that way," Reed said. "But I'm afraid it wouldn't take much to get the whole thing sliding again."

"What would we use? We'd have to have a generator to run a skill saw," Dad said.

"I've got a chain saw," Brother Bennion told them.

"That would work," Reed said. "It might buck more than a skill saw, though, and shake everything loose."

"What choice do we have?" Brother Bennion asked.

"I hate to take that kind of time." Dad thought for a moment. Then he walked along the house, knelt, and looked under the roof again. "I think I can crawl under right here. Maybe while you round up a saw, I can take my first-aid kit and work my way inside. I might be able to stop some bleeding and buy them a little time that way."

Reed shook his head. "If we start cutting an opening and the place gives way, I don't want you in there."

"Okay. Until then, I'll go in and see what I can find out. If they're already gone, we'll know. If they're not, I'll do what I can and then get out."

"What if we get another aftershock?"

Dad looked around. "Did the house slide when that last shock hit?"

"I don't know," Brother Davidson said. "I don't think so. But that wasn't a hard one. If we got a really good one, I'm not sure what might happen."

"I think I'd better go in," Reed said. "I'm smaller than you are."

Brother Dayley, who had been silent until now, said, "I'm smaller than either one of you. Why don't you let me go in?"

"I'd rather do it," Dad said. "I've got the first-aid training. Bill, what you might do is finish checking the rest of the houses on this street and get a report back to the bishop. Could someone run and get my first-aid kit from Julie?"

"I will," a man said and took off running.

Lucky was worried. He didn't want his dad to do this. He stepped closer, leaned against his dad's side. "It could cave in some more," he said softly.

"I don't think so. I think it's down as far as it's going to go. I'll be all right."

Dad knelt and looked again, flashing the light around in different directions. "I can see a pretty good opening right through here. I can at least get in far enough to see whether there's any chance of finding them."

It was another minute or so before the man got back with the first-aid kit. Then, before Dad could get started, a man came around the house and said, "Who's got any bandages? We pulled Brother Carver out, and he's got a big gash on his head."

Dad swung around. "I need to take this kit of mine inside. Tyler, can you help with that?"

"Yeah. I checked. I've got one big compress."

"Have you got a stretch bandage?"

"Yeah."

"Okay. Put the compress on him, and tighten it down with that stretch bandage. Don't wrap it too tight, but get it nice and snug so it stops the bleeding. Lucky, you go and help him."

Lucky didn't want to leave his dad, but he went. He doubted Tyler knew what he was doing. He and Tyler followed the man to the front yard of the house next to the Hamptons.

Brother Carver was sitting on the grass. Several people were crowded around him. He was a big, older man who had a bald spot in the back of his gray hair. His hair was matted with blood now, and he was moaning softly, seemingly stunned.

Tyler knelt by him and said, "Are you hurt anywhere else, besides your head?"

"I hurt all over," Brother Carver moaned.

"Where exactly?"

"I don't know. My knee. My ankle."

"He probably twisted his leg," a man next to Tyler said. "He might have broken something."

"What about your chest?" Tyler said. "Or your back?"

"I don't know," Brother Carver mumbled again. "Where's Lucille?"

"She's all right," a woman said. "We've got her wrapped in blankets over here. She hurt her shoulder a little, but she's just fine."

"All right," Tyler said. "We'll stop this bleeding, and then we'll keep you still until we can get some more help. Don't try to move."

Lucky was amazed. Tyler seemed to know what he was talking about. He watched as Tyler inspected the wound on Brother Carver's head. "It's not as bad as it looks," he announced. "The head just bleeds a lot."

He got out some disinfectant in a tube, squeezed some onto his finger, and rubbed it into the wound. Brother Carver winced, but Tyler talked to him softly.

Then he placed the bandage over the wound and wrapped the stretch bandage around his head to tighten it down, just as Dad had said.

By then, someone had brought a couple of blankets. "Let's get him down," Tyler said, and he told Brother Carver, "Let us move you. If anything hurts, stop us."

Slowly Tyler and a man and woman helped lower him back onto the blanket, and then they lifted him enough to pull the blanket down under his legs.

"Shouldn't we keep his legs up?" the woman asked.

"Not with a head wound," Tyler said. "We need to elevate his head a little.

By then, someone was putting another blanket over Brother Carver, and a young woman said she would run and get a pillow. It was only then that Lucky realized it was Celeste.

While she was gone, Lucky pulled his jacket off and put it under Brother Carver's head and shoulders. All the while, Tyler kept talking to Brother Carver, trying to comfort him. Lucky was surprised to know that Tyler could be that gentle—but not so surprised as he would have been had he seen this the day before.

Lucky heard someone approaching, and then he recognized Julie's voice. "Do we need to get him to a hospital?"

"I don't know," Tyler said, and some of his confidence seemed to diminish once he knew a nurse was there. "He might have a broken ankle."

"We better just keep him here for now," Julie said. "Even if we could get him to the hospital, that place is going to be a mess with all the people coming in. We're keeping Sister Steele here for now, too. She's conscious now, and she seems to be doing all right."

Julie knelt and inspected Tyler's work. "Good job," she said. Then she asked, "Brother Carver, how are you feeling? Does that ankle hurt much?"

"I don't know," Brother Carver mumbled. "Not too much, I guess."

"Maybe we can put a splint on it. But you just rest for right now." She looked over at Lucky. "Are the Hamptons still inside?"

"Yeah," Lucky said. "My dad's trying to get into them."

"Well, we need to give them our attention, if the men can get them out. Afterward, we'll look at all the little things." She looked up. "Is anyone else hurt?"

"My daughter cut her arm," a woman said. "I did the best I could with it. You might want to look at it."

Julie stood up and walked over to the woman, who was holding her little daughter in her arms.

Celeste showed up about then with the pillow. Tyler lifted Brother Carver a little. Lucky pulled his jacket out, and Celeste worked the pillow under Brother Carver.

Tyler said, "Just rest now," and then all fell silent. Lucky could hear the men next door moving about and talking, but he couldn't tell what was happening. He wondered whether his dad was inside yet.

"You guys did a great job," a woman said quietly.

"Tyler did," Lucky told her.

He felt Celeste touch his shoulder. "You both did," she said.

Lucky was surprisingly warmed by that, even though he hadn't done much of anything.

Lucky wished the sun would come up. He could hear sirens somewhere in the distance. He wished there were some way to get an ambulance up to Brother Carver and Sister Steele. What if these head injuries were really serious? Both of them needed to be in a hospital, not lying outside on their front lawns.

Lucky was still kneeling by Brother Carver. He looked off the hill, and now he could see that more fires were burning. He counted five, one of them really quite large. Lucky saw the flash of emergency lights on a distant street, but no other lights. He glanced up at the sky and saw that, with the town so dark, the stars were stunningly bright. Somehow it seemed strange that the stars would look so calm and quiet in the sky when underneath the earth had turned so violent.

In a short time a pickup truck came down the street and pulled into the the Hamptons' driveway. Lucky thought it was Brother Bennion. Whoever the man was, he got out and stepped around to the back of the truck. He lifted something out—probably a saw.

Lucky couldn't stand not knowing what his dad was doing, so he walked back to the Hamptons. "What's going on? What's my dad doing?" he called to the man who had gotten out of the truck.

"I'm not sure. He must be inside by now. But you'd better stay back." Lucky could see now for sure that he was talking with Brother Bennion.

Lucky walked to the back of the house in spite of what he had been told. He could see Reed, kneeling by the back of the house, shining a light under the end of the roof. "Is my dad inside?" Lucky asked.

"Yeah. But he's having trouble getting through. We're probably going to have to cut our way in."

"I've got the saw ready," Brother Bennion said.

"Stay where you are for right now," Reed said. That only worried Lucky more. It meant that Reed thought things were still unstable.

Lucky waited. His breath seemed to be caught in his chest. He just wanted his dad out of there.

Then he heard Reed shout, "You might as well come back out then. We'll cut an opening and get inside. We might have to brace everything before we take any chances."

That sounded good. Lucky waited and watched for his dad to crawl back out.

Suddenly Lucky felt the vibration. A second after that, a hard shock cracked through the ground like a little explosion. The earth seemed to ripple under him.

Lucky heard the sound at the same time that he saw Reed jump back and scramble down the hill. There was a terrific knock, as though something had dropped, hitting hard, and then Lucky heard boards creaking and snapping. Everything was giving way, sliding down the hill.

Lucky jumped back instinctively, but at the same time he shouted, "Oh no! Oh no!"

The rumble lasted for only a few seconds, then everything stopped again. Nothing but silence. Lucky couldn't see how far things had slid.

Flashlights began to slash through the darkness, and men started to shout.

"Ron! Ron!" Lucky heard Reed yell as the man scrambled back up the hill. "Can you hear me? Are you all right?"

Lucky worked his way farther down the hill. He was getting nothing more than quick images, but he could tell that the roof of the house had held together and slid maybe ten feet farther down the hill. He had no idea what was happening inside.

"Is he answering?" another voice shouted.

The first voice, Reed's, came back, "No. He's not responding. We've got to get in there. Get that chain saw down here. We're going to have to cut an opening in the roof now."

Lucky didn't know what to do. He stood, waiting, unable to move. This just couldn't happen.

"They'll get him out," Tyler said behind him.

Lucky didn't know. He couldn't talk. He couldn't even think. He didn't want to accept the possibilities.

Lucky began walking closer, hardly aware of what he was doing. He heard the motor on the chain saw catch, and then it began to putt. At the same time one of the men, Brother Davidson, came toward him out of the dark. "Move back. The house could shift again."

About then Brother Davidson realized he was talking to Lucky. "Don't worry. He'll be all right," he added.

The chain saw screeched and bucked as it bit into the roofing. Two men were holding flashlights, and Reed was cutting. But the progress was unbelievably slow. Lucky was afraid another earthquake would hit and everything would go down the side of the hill—the men and the house, with Dad in the middle of it all. Or maybe just the cutting would break things loose.

Sparks flashed as the saw struck a nail, and for a moment Lucky could see the intensity in the men's faces. Reed cut a vertical line about four feet long. Then he turned the saw ninety degrees and drove it into the roof again. This time, he must have hit a beam. The saw seemed to stop.

Minutes kept going by. Lucky kept seeing his dad, crushed under some terrible weight, struggling to breathe, bleeding. Thinking about it was too awful, but why else had he not called back? He had to be hurt—and hurt bad.

Eventually Reed set the saw down, and the men pulled a section of roof away. Lucky's breath held as Reed stepped forward and grabbed a flashlight from one of the men. Then he ducked inside.

"Hurry, hurry," Lucky finally said out loud.

"They'll get him out," Tyler said.

Lucky heard Celeste's voice. "He's big and strong," she said. "He'll be okay."

She took hold of his arm, but Lucky hardly realized that. "Hurry. Hurry," he kept saying.

Chapter 9

Give me the saw!" Lucky heard Reed yell from inside, under the roof, and a few moments later the saw screamed again as it began to cut. The noise lasted only a few seconds, however, and then Reed threw something out. Lucky couldn't see what it was.

The darkness kept Lucky from seeing anything clearly. Another man stepped inside, and then some debris, dark and indefinable, flew from the opening. He expected any second that everything would give way again and that Reed and the others would be hurt this time.

They were talking constantly, and Lucky heard bits of their conversation. "Don't cut that—it's supporting all the weight." And then a minute later, "Push on that two-by-six. Will it move?"

Lucky couldn't picture what was happening inside, but he knew they were being careful—and working frantically at the same time. He thought an hour had gone by before he heard Reed shout, "Okay, I've got him. He's alive."

Lucky felt a sob of relief break loose inside him, and he realized he had been holding his breath.

"He's got a lot of weight on him, though." Reed paused and then shouted, "Is there a jack in your truck, Dan?"

Brother Bennion answered, "Yeah. I'll get it."

More time was slipping by. Lucky hated to think what might happen if the men started jacking things up. But the greater terror was that they couldn't get the weight off his dad, that he would just have to lie there and die.

Brother Bennion ran to his truck and back, and after that Lucky heard only muffled voices. Finally someone yelled, "Stay back out there. We're going to jack this up now."

Lucky heard another voice say, "Take it slow now."

That was the last thing Lucky wanted to hear. A creaking noise followed, and Lucky held his breath once again. He could hear the noise begin and stop, begin again. Each time he heard the voices inside, under the dark roof.

Then came a painfully long silence. Lucky expected any minute for someone to say, "He's dead." Somewhere deep inside him was a memory, a moment of truth, when his mother finally stopped breathing. Lucky had thought he had been prepared, but he hadn't been. He felt the same sense now, that he may have to accept this again, but he just knew he couldn't do it.

He didn't really say any of those things to himself though. He kept clinging to the idea that somehow everything had to be all right. "Please don't let him die," he kept saying in his mind. "Please, Heavenly Father, please."

At last he saw movement. A man was climbing slowly out of the opening in the roof. A little light hit him, and Lucky saw that he was stepping backward, hefting a heavy load. The men were bringing his dad out.

Lucky couldn't stand it any longer. He ran to them, yelling "Dad! Dad! Can you hear me?"

Four men had hold of Brother Ladd. Reed grunted, "Stay back. Let's get him away from this house."

"Is he alive?"

"Yeah. He's breathing."

"Can he hear me?"

"I don't think so."

The men trudged around the house and up the steep hillside, struggling with the weight. By the time they reached the front lawn, they were breathing hard. But they were careful to set Dad down carefully.

"It wasn't good to move him like that," Reed said

to Lucky. "He could have a back injury. But we didn't have any choice. We had to get him out of there."

Lucky leaned close to his dad's face. "Dad! Dad!" His father didn't respond, and his breathing seemed very soft.

Julie knelt down by Ron Ladd. "Could you see any injuries?" she asked. She felt his throat for his pulse.

"He took a blow on the back of the head," Reed answered. "That's the only thing I could see. The weight was across his chest and his stomach."

"His pulse is fairly strong right now," Julie said. "But he could have internal injuries. We need to get him to the hospital somehow. He needs a CAT scan and some tests. He might need surgery." She gave his face a little slap. "Ron! Listen to me. Can you hear me?"

He showed no response.

Lucky was still leaning close. He felt some comfort in the steady breathing. But his dad's face looked pasty white under the flashlights.

"We'd better get him in the back of the truck and drive him down to the hospital," Brother Bennion said.

Lucky wanted that. He wanted doctors. He wanted someone who could find out what was wrong—someone who could do something. He felt a hand on his back, patting him, and he heard Celeste's voice. "He'll be okay, Lucky."

"How do we know the hospital held together?" someone asked.

It was a chilling question.

"If it didn't, there will still be staff down there, working outside, or whatever," Julie said. "I can't do anything for him here."

"The streets might be bad. I'll run and get my four-wheeler," Brother Davidson said and sprinted off. Lucky knew he lived just across the street.

"Does someone have a board? And a blanket?" Julie shouted. Other people took off running.

Time was passing, though, and Lucky knew time had to be an enemy. Somehow someone had to do something before it was too late. "Shouldn't someone give him a blessing?" Lucky asked.

"I was just thinking the same thing," Reed said.

"Dad keeps a little bottle of consecrated oil in his first-aid kit." Lucky was already searching through the kit.

Reed helped him, and they found the oil, and then Brother Bennion anointed Brother Ladd's head, and Reed said the blessing. "Father, please spare this good man. He's still needed here upon the earth. Keep him alive until we can get him some help."

Lucky felt better having heard the words, but when he looked at his father, he still saw little sign of life.

Headlights were already coming up the street,

however, and then the big four-wheel Blazer turned and backed into the driveway. Reed and Julie had begun to fashion a stretcher from a blanket and a board.

Lucky had to get out of the way while they worked it under his dad, and then four men lifted his father up and put him into the back end of the Blazer. Lucky jumped in the back with his dad, and Julie climbed in next to him.

Reed climbed in the front with Brother Davidson, and someone closed the back of the Blazer. Then they were rolling. Brother Davidson took it easy. Lucky knew he had to watch the road carefully. It was all so slow. At least the hospital was only a few blocks away.

As Brother Davidson turned left at the bottom of the hill, however, Reed said, "Oh, no. Look at the police lights. They've got the bridge blocked off."

"It must have gone out," Brother Davidson replied. He pulled to the side of the street and made a U-turn. "Where can we get across the river?"

"They rebuilt the bridge over on Columbia Lane. Maybe that one held together."

Lucky had thought they were just a minute or so from the hospital, but now he wondered. Maybe there was no getting across the Provo River. Maybe all the bridges were down. What would they do then?

Brother Davidson headed back onto Grandview Hill, this time driving much faster. He drove north, across the hill, and turned east again, but as he started down the steep hill toward Columbia Lane, a man suddenly appeared in the headlights. He was waving his arms.

Lucky stretched to see what the problem was this time. He heard the man say, "There's a big break in the road up there. You can't drive through it."

"Now what?" Brother Davidson asked. He turned back again and headed past Grandview Elementary.

"Turn north up here at the first corner," Reed said. "I think we can get over to State Street, there by the Minuteman. We should be able to get down the State Street hill. That big bridge should be all right."

Brother Davidson cut right, and then right again. All the while Dad was breathing, though weakly. Lucky wished he could hear a groan or see his dad move a finger. But he saw nothing. And time was moving on. What if he was bleeding inside all this time? How much longer could he last?

State Street was wide open, and Brother Davidson accelerated down the hill. The bridge was all right, too, but at the big intersection at the bottom of the hill, water was running across the road. "A water main must have broken down here," Brother Davidson said.

He slowed, and Lucky worried that they would be stopped again. The truck, however, pushed on through the water, which wasn't very deep. Then they were moving fast again. The hospital was just up ahead.

Brother Davidson turned left, and then right. Lucky saw a sign ahead that said, "Emergency."

He could also see that an ambulance was in the entrance, and behind it were a couple of cars and a truck. The Blazer wouldn't be able to pull all the way in.

"Drive in as far as you can, and I'll run for help," Reed said.

And that's what he did. He didn't return quickly, though. Lucky had thought everything would be all right once they made it to the hospital. Now he could see that the place was in a mess. Another truck pulled in behind the Blazer, and a man jumped out and ran.

At the door to the emergency room, a number of people were crowded around, and a policeman was talking to them. Reed was only one of them. Several seconds later, Reed went into the hospital.

"This could be bad," Julie whispered. "I hope enough doctors have gotten down here. Things could turn into chaos before long."

Brother Davidson got out of the truck and came around to open the back. Lucky jumped down as soon as he did. Unable to stand the wait, he ran to the emergency entrance. He wanted to tell the policeman that someone had to help his dad. About then two men in white, with a gurney, came out the glass doors and hurried in Lucky's direction. Reed was with them.

Julie and Brother Davidson worked from inside, and the paramedics—or whatever they were—from the outside. In only a few seconds, Dad was on the gurney, heading inside.

At the emergency entrance Lucky heard the policeman say, "Sir, you'll have to take care of that yourself for right now. The doctors are dealing only with life-threatening injuries."

But the man was angry. "She's cut—really deep. It's got to be sewn up."

Lucky heard no more. He walked beside the gurney, but Reed stopped at the door. "You go with him for now, Julie," Reed said. "Randy and I need to get back to the hill. I still don't know where the Hamptons are in all that mess. I doubt they're alive."

The emergency room was clogged. Doctors and nurses were all over the place. They were trying to be systematic, but everything was in a state of confusion.

Lucky heard a woman shouting, "But she's in terrible pain. You have to do something."

A nurse was talking patiently, "I know, ma'am. Lots of people are in pain. But some could die. We have to look after them first."

"Just give her something for the pain!" the woman demanded.

"We will. Honestly, we will. We'll get to her as soon as we can."

Lucky heard all this, saw the crazy scene around him, but very little of it was registering. He could only see his father, looking much too white, seeming hardly to breathe, lying absolutely motionless.

"This man is serious, Dr. Greenwell," Julie told a doctor who was just inside the entrance doors. "Head injury. Possible internal injuries. His pulse is slowing down."

Lucky hadn't known that. He took a deep breath and hoped that someone would do something right away.

"Take this one. Stat," the doctor yelled.

Suddenly Dad's gurney was shooting on through the room, being pulled by a nurse and a man in a green "scrub" outfit. Lucky hoped the man was a doctor.

Lucky followed, although no one seemed to notice him. Once the gurney was inside a little curtained area, the doctor went to work, listening to his dad's heart, getting some sort of monitors hooked to him. The nurse was setting up an IV and getting the needle into Dad's arm.

Lucky watched as long as he could stand it before he said, "Is he going to be okay?"

The doctor glanced over, seeming to notice Lucky for the first time. "Are you his son?"

"Yes."

"Stay back a little. I don't know much yet. We'll find out. And we'll do all we can."

"He took a blow on the back of his head," Julie told the man. "And he had a lot of weight across his chest and abdomen."

The doctor nodded. After that, he didn't say anything. Lucky felt hope draining from him. His dad looked terrible, like a lump of blue flesh, not even human anymore. And it all reminded him of his mother.

"Father in Heaven," he whispered again, "please don't let him die too." He had already said it a hundred times. Two hundred. Five hundred. But in the back of his mind was a haunting memory: he had prayed for his mother too. Over and over and over. And she had died anyway.

Dad had always given Lucky explanations for all that. And Lucky had managed to live with them. But this was different. This was too much.

"Please don't let him die. Please," he kept whispering.

"We need to do a CAT scan," the doctor told another man—possibly another doctor. "Something is going on inside, maybe a ruptured spleen. His blood pressure is in the basement. I think we're going to have to open him up and find out."

"Okay. Let's take him. Harvey Spendlove just came in the door. He can do the surgery."

Then one of the doctors looked at Julie. "Can you help out front?" he said. "We don't have enough nurses."

"All right." She patted Lucky on the head. "These guys are good," she told him. "They'll take care of him. Okay?"

Lucky nodded, but he hated the idea of being alone.

He had to stand back, and no one would tell him what was happening. One of the doctors hooked up some electric wires to Dad's head and then watched a monitor. "What does that mean?" Lucky asked, but the doctor only said, "It's too soon to tell."

And then Dad was moving again. Down a long hallway. A young man in the same green hospital clothes as the doctors' was pushing him. Lucky followed. "Are you with him?" the man asked.

Lucky nodded.

"Look," the orderly said, "no one's going to be able to be with you. It's just a mess. You can wait outside the operating room. When I get a chance, I'll let you know what's happening."

"Is he going to live?"

"I'm sorry. I really don't know. Did they tell you what's wrong with him?" The boy was maybe twenty, with long hair and a stubble of a beard. Lucky thought he had a nice voice—gentle. He did seem to care.

"Not really. Something about a ruptured spleen."

"They'll take good care of him, I'll tell you that. Where's your mom?"

"She . . . uh . . . died. A couple of years ago."

"Oh, brother. Hey, I'm sorry. I'll tell them to do a good job. Okay? You wait out here." They had reached the entrance to the operating room. The young man pushed the gurney in, and Lucky was left standing in a half-dark waiting room. No one else was there.

Lucky didn't move. He just waited like a statue, and in a couple of minutes or so the young man came out, pushing the empty gurney. "They'll fix him. Don't worry. Spendlove is a good surgeon. He'll take care of everything."

"Does he know what's wrong?"

"Not yet. They have to open him up and find out."

"He isn't dead, is he? He looked dead."

"No. I mean, he's—you know—not in real good shape. But they'll do everything they can."

Lucky had heard that before. Doctors had always said that about his mother. He walked over and sat down on a couch as the orderly wheeled the gurney away. Lucky sat stiffly on the front edge, staring straight ahead. Finally he asked himself the question, What would happen to him if his dad died?

He would live with Grandma and Grandpa, Lucky supposed. The image was not so terrible, but then he thought of his dad's big laugh, and all the joking and the fun, him hugging Lucky with those big bear arms.

Lucky finally sat back on the couch, covered his face with his hands, and cried.

Chapter 10

*T*he waiting room soon began to fill up. More and more gurneys rolled into the operating room, and relatives gathered in the waiting area, which was near the front entrance to the hospital. Some asked Lucky how he was doing. He said very little, though. He didn't want to talk. He kept watching for that guy—the young one—to ask how things were going. Or for the doctor, who would maybe come out and tell him how his dad was doing. Or for Julie, who could maybe go in and ask. But an hour went by, and Lucky didn't hear a word, didn't see anyone he knew.

He thought of calling his grandparents, but he didn't want to scare them. Then he found out the phones weren't working anyway. Lots of things weren't working. The hospital had its own generators, but a woman came through and asked people to leave most of the lights off to conserve energy. She said the hospi-

tal had taken some damage, but none of the patients
was seriously hurt.

Lucky wished his grandparents were there with
him. By now someone must have let them know what
had happened. Maybe they would show up before long.

Then Lucky looked over toward the glass doors at
the front of the hospital. Tyler had just walked in. He
was looking around the room, obviously scanning for
Lucky. Lucky stood up and walked over to him. Tyler
looked tired—and dirty. He had on an old Levi jacket,
but he had gotten something white—or gray—all over
it. And there was a big, dark smudge across his cheek.

"How's your dad doing?" Tyler asked as Lucky
approached.

"I don't know. They're operating on him."

"Where's he hurt?"

"They didn't know."

"Are you okay?"

Lucky shrugged. He swallowed, held on for a
moment, got under control, and then said, "How'd you
get down here?"

"Walked."

"Really? How did you get across the river?"

"The bridge isn't down. It's just cracked and sort of
twisted. They aren't letting cars on it. But they're letting people walk across—if they have to." He hesitated.

"My mom tried to drive down—but she got stopped. She sent me over to see what I could find out."

Lucky nodded. She had to be worried.

"She talked to your grandma," Tyler said, "and she's really worried."

"Did anyone get the Hamptons out yet?" Lucky asked.

"No. But someone got inside far enough to find them. They were both dead. Everything came right down on top of them."

It crossed Lucky's mind that his dad had gone in to save the Hamptons' lives when it was already too late. He didn't want to think about that. "Is anyone else hurt up there?"

"Sister Steele is doing okay, I think. I heard someone in the fourth ward got hurt really bad too—and might die—but I don't know who it was."

Lucky had the feeling that there were things he ought to say to Tyler, but he didn't know quite how to go about it. Instead, the two of them walked over toward the couches where Lucky had been sitting. All the seats, however, had been taken, so they just stood, no longer facing each other.

"I don't want to walk back yet," Tyler said. "If I tell my mom they don't know what's going on, she'll just worry all the more."

Lucky nodded. "I wish someone would come out

and say something," he said, and his voice cracked a little. He felt Tyler shift his weight a little, sort of bump up against Lucky, arm to arm.

They stood like that for a couple of minutes before Tyler said, "Your dad's fighting hard. That's how he is. He'll probably be okay." He took a breath and added, "My dad just quit on me."

Now it was Tyler's voice that had squeezed off. And Lucky was the one who leaned ever so slightly against Tyler's shoulder.

"Have you heard anything from him?" Lucky asked.

"No."

"Does anyone know where this earthquake hit? Was this the center of it, or what?"

"I heard it hit downtown Salt Lake really bad too. The freeway is supposed to be a big mess. A lot of the overpasses are down. People were listening to the radio. They said a parking garage fell in, somewhere in downtown Salt Lake, and I guess one big apartment house broke up and killed a bunch of people."

"What about Provo?"

"The guy on the radio said that most of the old downtown buildings fell down. The city building too, where the police station is—I guess that took a lot of damage."

"I saw some fires," Lucky said.

"Yeah. There are fires all over the place. Some

really big ones in Salt Lake are out of control. And there were some big rock slides in the canyons."

"What about the houses way up on the mountain?"

"I don't know. I haven't heard anything about that. I guess the dam up at Deer Creek is okay. But they're telling people in the river bottoms to clear out—just in case."

"Everything's going to be a big mess for a long time."

"I know. Our school is about halfway knocked down. Someone said we won't have any school the rest of the year."

Lucky was disheartened to hear that. Everything was going to be different now. He continued to keep his eyes on the door to the operating room. Under everything else, the words kept repeating themselves: "Please, God, don't let him die."

"I'm sorry I hit you yesterday."

"What?" Lucky couldn't think what Tyler meant for a moment. "Oh. Was that yesterday?" Lucky felt his lip and was surprised to know that it was still swollen. It was even sore, now that he thought about. "That seems like a month ago."

"I know." Another pause followed, but Tyler wasn't finished. "I'm sorry I said that stuff about your dad. He's a good guy. I just . . . you know . . . "

"Yeah. I know."

All this didn't really matter now, though. Lucky focused on the door and waited. And prayed. He could deal with anything else, but Dad had to live.

All the same, time kept going by. And no one came out to tell him anything. Lucky wondered whether anyone would. Things were so crazy. Maybe Dad had died an hour ago, and no one knew Lucky was waiting.

Then someone touched his shoulder, and he turned around to see Carol—with Kristin and Heather and Molly. They all looked sort of thrown together, in sweat shirts and old jeans and with their hair sort of messy. They all looked worried too.

"What's happening?" Carol asked.

"I don't know," Lucky said. "He's in the operating room. He's been in there about two hours, or something like that. I've lost track of time."

"Do they know how serious it is?"

"They didn't even know what was wrong."

"Oh, Lucky," Carol said, and her eyes filled with tears. Lucky felt the tears well up in his own eyes, but he tried not to cry.

"He'll be okay," Kristin said, and she stepped over and put her arm around Lucky's shoulder.

Lucky thought that was a stupid thing to say. Kristin didn't know that parents could die. She hadn't seen this stuff, the way Lucky had. Lucky held stiff when she tried to pull him close against her side.

"I don't even know if they remember I'm out here," Lucky said. "Something might have happened already." And that brought the tears spilling onto his cheeks.

"No, no. I'm sure they would come out and tell you," Carol said. But Lucky saw the concern in her face deepen.

Heather and Molly were wide-eyed and frightened. They were both clinging to their mother's legs, on opposite sides. Lucky understood why they were here. They hadn't wanted to be separated from their mother.

"How did you get down here, Mom?" Tyler asked.

"I drove clear around. The State Street bridge is the only one they'll let you cross." She looked at Lucky. "I talked to your grandparents, Lucky, but I didn't tell them that it was serious. I didn't know for sure, and I didn't want to worry them. I told them I'd come down and check on him, and then let them know."

Lucky nodded. He thought about having to tell his grandparents if Dad didn't make it. Poor Grandma would never be able to handle it. She had been through enough already.

Lucky looked past Carol and saw a doctor in a green scrub outfit come through the doors from the operating room. He was looking around. Lucky pushed past Carol and hurried toward him.

"Ladd?" he said.

"Yes."

The doctor looked serious, sort of sad, and Lucky knew what that meant. Lucky's heart seemed to burst inside. He didn't want to hear the words.

Carol was suddenly there, grasping Lucky's shoulders. And she too must have seen it in the doctor's eyes. Lucky felt the desperation in her grasp.

"We've done all we can do," the doctor said.

A sob broke from Lucky. It's what doctors always said.

"I think he's got a pretty good chance. But I can't promise anything. His liver was lacerated, and we sutured the capsule around it. That isn't going to be a big problem. But he took a very serious blow to the head. He's got a cerebral bleed—a small area where he's bleeding into his brain."

He was talking mostly to Carol, probably assuming she was Lucky's mother. Lucky asked, "What does that do?"

"Well, the big problem comes twelve to twenty-four hours later—from what we call cerebral edema. That's swelling of the brain. There's just no predicting how serious that might be. I'd say, if he gets through the first twenty-four hours all right, then he should make it."

"Will his brain be messed up?"

The doctor sort of cocked his head to one side, as if to say, "Yeah, maybe." But he said, "He *could* have some paralysis. He could also recover completely. It just depends on how bad the swelling is and where the pressure is."

The doctor was a thin man, an older man. He sounded tired, and something in his voice didn't offer much hope. "Aren't you his wife?" he asked Carol.

"No," she said. "This is his son."

The doctor bent forward a little and looked into Lucky's eyes. "They told me he was trying to save someone's life—get someone out of a house."

Lucky nodded.

"Well, he's a brave man. And he's a fighter. He could have died very easily, as hard a blow as he took. But he's a strong man, and he's hanging in there. So maybe he'll be all right. Don't give up hope."

Lucky nodded again.

"Where's your mom?"

Lucky couldn't say it. So Carol explained. "She died a few years ago."

Lucky saw the pain come into the doctor's eyes. "Well, we'll keep after this thing. We'll watch him close. I wish . . . you know . . . that I could promise. But I can't. I will make sure you find out what's going on. We're taking him over to ICU—Intensive Care—so you might want to keep in touch with the people over there. You might be better off to go home for a while— if you still have one."

"I want to stay here," Lucky said.

The doctor nodded. Then he looked at Carol, but he didn't ask who she was. "Is your home all right?" he asked.

"Well . . . it's not too bad, I guess."

"Mine's a mess. We live in Sherwood Hills, on the mountainside. Things really rumbled up there. Some of the houses came right off the mountain. Mine sort of hung together, but it's all twisted and cracked. I don't think we can salvage much of it."

Lucky couldn't believe it. The man had just worked for two hours on his dad while, more than anything, he must have been worrying about his own family, his own tragedy. "Thanks," Lucky said, unable to say all that was on his mind.

The doctor patted his head one more time and left.

Carol still had her arm around Lucky's shoulders. And now Tyler and the girls gathered in front of them. Kristin smiled and said, "Lucky, I have a really good feeling that he's going to be all right. I've been praying . . . and—"

Her voice broke, and she started to cry. At the same time, he felt Carol begin to shake, and he knew she was crying too. Molly and Heather had tears in their eyes, and Tyler was looking solemn, worried. Lucky couldn't seem to stop his own tears, but he was glad that at least he wasn't alone now.

Chapter 11

Lucky and the Wakefields walked to the ICU waiting room. They hadn't been there long before Carol said, "Lucky, maybe we ought to go home for a while. There's nothing we can do here right now."

"I want to stay."

"I know you do. So do I, in a way. But it might be better if we get out of here for a while. For one thing, we need to talk to your grandparents."

Lucky knew that was true. So he agreed to go, but he said he wanted to come back soon—and stay during the night.

"Well, let's see what your grandparents want you to do about that."

Lucky didn't know what they would say. He just knew he didn't want to be away from the hospital for very long. Still, he left with the Wakefields.

They took the long way home, up State Street and

then back around to Grandview Hill, but they could travel better now, in the light. Along the way Lucky could see more of the damage than he had before.

Most homes had held together, but bricks had fallen off some of them, and lots of chimneys had shaken apart. Lucky could see all kinds of damage: broken windows, car ports down on top of cars, open breaks in the street. What he noticed most were all the people. They were setting up to stay outside—pitching tents in their yards, making breakfast on Coleman stoves. It was all like a mass camp out.

Lucky found his grandma and grandpa out in the RV. They were relieved to see Lucky and the Wakefields when they came through the door, but Grandma began to cry when they heard the news, and Grandpa turned pale.

Grandma took Lucky in her arms. "Oh, Lucky, after all this traveling around, how could he come home and get hurt? He just has to get better. I can't stand it if he doesn't."

Grandpa put his hands on their shoulders. "Don't talk that way," he told her gently. "We'll stand what we have to stand."

He sounded like Dad.

Lucky had been home for only a few minutes when Uncle Mitch and Willy showed up. Lucky had to explain again what was happening. Kristin added, "The doctor said if he gets through the next twenty-four hours, he should be all right."

Lucky didn't remember the words as quite that optimistic, but he didn't say so.

Uncle Mitch hugged Lucky, much like Dad's bear hugs. "He's a strong man," he said. "He's not going to be stopped by a little old house falling on him, I can tell you that."

Lucky liked to think of it that way—to think how strong and stubborn his dad was. But he also knew that Dad was hurt inside, and in his head. Maybe it didn't matter how strong he was.

Lucky sat down on the little couch, and Willy sat down next to him. "He just needs some fresh air," Willy said, trying to lighten things a little. But he couldn't bring himself to laugh, and Lucky couldn't either.

Tyler slid into the wrap-around seat at the kitchen table.

"I guess everyone knows about the Hamptons," Uncle Mitch said. "I just heard some other bad news. A house over on the north side of the hill burned down. The family got out, but one of the sons was burned really bad. They don't know if he's going to live."

"We heard on the radio that they've already counted over sixty deaths in Salt Lake, and quite a number in Ogden," Grandpa added. "If the earthquake had hit in the day time, they said it would have been thousands."

"Did you know the roof on the Marriott Center caved in?" Carol asked. "What if it had happened when it was full of people?"

Lucky was surprised to hear all this. How could any force be that powerful?

Grandpa said, "I talked to the bishop a little while ago. We've got a lot of people cut up and bruised and that sort of thing, but his big worry now is all the people who were evacuated out of the river bottoms."

"Where are they going to stay?" Uncle Mitch asked.

"Most of them are over on those soccer and baseball fields, by Westridge school. But they weren't given time to bring much of anything with them. They need to eat—and they'll need sleeping bags and all the rest if they end up staying the night. The stake president has asked the wards to start collecting food and bedding for them."

"What are we all going to do?" Grandma's voice quivered. She was fighting hard to keep control. "When will we get our lights back? When will we—"

Just then Lucky felt what everyone else felt: a little trembler, just big enough to notice.

Everyone hesitated, and then Mitch said, "Mom, we're alive. Our houses have a few problems, but they can be fixed. We'll get our power back in a few days. And we've got plenty of food. We'll be fine."

Everyone was looking very serious, but then little Molly said, "Mommy told us we can't go to the bath-room."

Uncle Mitch laughed almost as loudly as Dad would have. "You can just wait for a few days, can't you?" he asked.

"Uh, uh. I don't think so."

Then Uncle Mitch told her, "Well, we've got the RV—with a chemical toilet. We're lucky. Do you want to use it now?"

Molly nodded rather eagerly, and everyone laughed. Molly looked embarrassed, but when Grandma pointed the way, she hurried into the little room and shut the door.

"That's going to be a problem," Uncle Mitch said. "We're going to have to get some people together and start digging latrines. The plumbing isn't going to work until we get the water pressure back, and I understand that water mains are broken all over town. It could be a long time before we get running water back."

It was all so strange. When would life ever be nor-mal again?

"Listen, everybody needs to get something to eat," Grandma said. "I don't think anyone has had any breakfast."

"I can't eat," Carol said.

Lucky was thinking the same thing.

"Well, you have to eat," Uncle Mitch told her. "We're luckier than most. Ron has propane in his tank. We can cook in here. I'll run over to our place and rob the freezer before everything starts to melt. We can have us a real feast—if we can all get in here."

"The kids can eat outside," Grandpa said. "It'll be a picnic. Bring your family over."

"Boys," Mitch said. "Come with me. Help me carry this food back."

Lucky agreed to go, but mainly so he could try to hurry things along. He wanted to get back to the hospital.

When Uncle Mitch and the boys neared Willy's house, Lucky saw Erin and Celeste coming toward them. Erin was the one who asked, "How's your dad doing, Lucky?"

"I don't know for sure," Lucky replied. "We're waiting to find out."

Erin and Celeste looked as sober as he had ever seen them. They had that same shocked look in their eyes that everyone seemed to have—as though they could hardly believe that everything could change so suddenly and completely.

Celeste looked at Tyler. "I heard that Heather cut her foot."

Tyler nodded.

"About twenty people did that. Spencer, my little brother, did the same thing."

"I can't believe Brother and Sister Hampton died," Erin said. "I saw them yesterday. Brother Hampton was out working in his yard. He was joking around with me, the way he always did. He was so nice."

"We went over to the school," Celeste added. "One big part of it just shook apart. It's all down on the ground. The rest of it is cracked and everything. Dad said the whole thing will have to be torn down."

No one found any joy in that. Not even Erin could think to make a joke.

"It was so terrible when my bed started jumping around," Celeste said. "I tried to get out of bed and got thrown right on the floor. I thought a plane had crashed on our house or something."

"I thought someone was jumping on my bed," Willy said. "I said, 'Leave me alone. Get out of here.' I figured it was one of my sisters giving me a hard time or something."

They all told their stories. Except Lucky. His mind kept drifting back to the hospital. Maybe something had happened by now. He wanted to be there.

Nevertheless, Lucky had to wait until everyone had eaten. As it turned out, Carol and Uncle Mitch went too, while the kids stayed at the RV with Grandma and

Grandpa. Tyler and Willy wanted to go with Lucky, but Uncle Mitch told them that they were needed in the neighborhood. He told them to go check in with the bishop and see what they could do.

When Lucky got to the ICU waiting room, he was afraid of what he might hear. Uncle Mitch went straight to the woman at the desk. When he came back, he said, "Lucky, she said that you and I could go in and see him." He glanced at Carol and said, "Immediate family." She bit her lip and nodded. Then he asked Lucky, "Do you want to see him?"

Lucky nodded. He wanted to see his dad, but he was scared of what he might learn. Lucky walked alongside Uncle Mitch, who kept his big hand on Lucky's shoulder the way Dad would have done, as a nurse led them to Dad's bed.

Lucky hated what he saw. His dad didn't look like himself. He had tubes running in his arm and into his mouth. And wires were attached to his head. The worst part was how white he was. He didn't look like himself. He looked the way Lucky's mom had, lying in her casket. Everyone had said how nice she looked, but Lucky had thought she looked terrible.

Lucky stood stiff, hesitant to touch his dad.

"Has he responded at all?" Mitch asked the nurse.

"No. But his vital signs aren't too bad. That's about

all I know. You'd have to check with the doctor to find out any more than that."

"I know. I just . . . wondered."

"Nothing's normal around here, sir," she said. "Things are awfully confused."

Uncle Mitch nodded, and then he put his hand on her arm, exactly the way Dad always did when he talked to people. "Listen, I just appreciate that you're here. Did you get through it okay?"

The nurse's eyes filled with tears. "I don't really know. I was down here. I haven't been home. I'm single, and I guess my apartment's okay. But my parents live out in Lehi, and I can't get hold of them."

"Everyone's kind of in the same situation," Mitch said. He patted her arm.

So many people were suffering today. It was what Lucky and his dad had seen so many times. But the two of them had always arrived a few days later, when the worst was over.

Lucky knew what his dad would say: that this whole thing was really a blessing. It was a chance to learn something. Lucky was suddenly a little ashamed that he had been thinking mostly about himself all day.

When he and his uncle went back to the waiting room, Lucky sat down on a couch across from Carol. He noticed the other people more than he had before. A woman was sitting in the corner with her hands clasped together. She was staring at the floor. She was wearing sweats and slippers and what looked like her husband's big jacket. Lucky thought of walking over to her, the way his dad would have done. But Uncle Mitch was the one who did it.

He talked to her for a few minutes, and when he came back, he told Lucky and Carol, "She's got a little boy in there who's really banged up. Her husband was working a night shift, and she hasn't been able to get hold of him. She's worried about him too."

Carol said, "A doctor just came out and told that family over there that their grandfather died."

Lucky saw how the people were clinging to each other, crying. One woman must have been the man's wife—but she didn't seem old enough to be a grand-mother. A younger woman—her daughter, Lucky guessed—was holding her and talking to her. Both of them were crying. A man was kneeling down, talking to two little boys, who looked wide-eyed and confused.

Uncle Mitch sat down next to Lucky, but after just a few minutes he said, "I can't sit here. I need to get back to the neighborhood and help with some of the things that have to be done. The truth is, it won't do any good for any of us to wait here. It's going to be quite a while before we know anything."

"I want to stay," Lucky said.

Uncle Mitch thought for a moment. "Well, okay," he said. "I'll come back for you later today."

"I just want to stay until . . . I know something. I can sleep here tonight, on this couch."

"Lucky, that won't—"

"I'll stay with him," Carol said.

"Well, all right. But I'll check back with you later on." As Uncle Mitch got up and walked away, Carol looked across at Lucky. "I'll stay with you," she said. "As long as it takes."

"You don't have to. I'll be okay."

"No. I want to be here too."

Lucky saw it in her eyes. She would feel the loss almost as much as Lucky would if Dad didn't make it.

Lucky got up, walked over to the other couch, and sat down by her. She put her arm around him—which is what he hoped she would do. And they sat together. They didn't talk much. They just waited.

Lucky watched the other people in the room. All of them were worried. He heard bits and pieces of their stories in their conversations. "The doctor said the burns aren't too bad," he heard a man say. "But he got a lot of smoke in his lungs." Lucky watched the man's wife. Her face was smudged with soot, and Lucky saw tear lines running down her cheeks. She wasn't crying now, though she looked frightened.

A doctor came out and told a young couple that

their baby was "doing about as well as could be expected." The woman started to cry and asked, "But is she going to live?"

"It's hard to say" was all the doctor could tell her. "We'll do our best."

When the doctor was gone, the young husband held his wife in his arms, and both of them cried. The mother was shaking and sobbing and grasping her husband tight. "She's so little," she kept saying.

So much pain. So many people suffering. Lucky was still praying, but he started adding more people to his prayers. The woman over in the corner, all alone. The couple with the burned child. The young couple. Even the family that had left—the one whose grandfather had been killed. As Lucky prayed, he thought how many more people there must be in Provo and Salt Lake and all the other towns in the area. He doubted there was a home without some damage, a family without some sort of worry. He hoped people had enough food.

The day was long and tedious, and Lucky heard more stories. Every now and then Lucky or Carol would ask the woman at the desk whether anything had changed. Each time she would say patiently, "I'll tell you the minute I know anything."

But nothing happened, and the long wait continued.

Chapter 12

Uncle Mitch came back with sandwiches late in the afternoon, but he couldn't talk Lucky—or Carol—into coming home. Mitch did say that Grandma and Grandpa and the girls were set up to sleep in the RV that night. He and the boys were going to sleep in tents.

Carol protested that her girls could sleep in a tent all right, but Mitch said it was all arranged.

After he left, the hours continued to drag. Lucky eventually curled up on the couch next to Carol and, after a restless time, fell asleep. He woke up a lot during the night, and each time he did, he looked at Carol, who was leaning back, trying to rest. But she never did seem to go to sleep.

It was almost morning and Lucky was only half asleep when he heard his name. "Is the Ladd boy still here?"

Lucky jumped up. He could hardly think where he was for a moment. A new woman was at the desk. She motioned for him to come over.

And Lucky knew.

He would have to give up his dad. It had happened. Lucky's chest turned to stone. He didn't think he could stand this.

He walked to the woman, with Carol by his side.

The woman was nodding as though she wanted to encourage him. What did that mean?

"The doctor told me to tell you that your dad is awake. He seems to be responding quite well."

For maybe one full second Lucky couldn't think what that meant, and then everything broke inside him. He spun to Carol and grasped her around the middle. "Thank God," Carol was saying.

And Lucky did thank God. "Thank you. Thank you. Thank you," he whispered between sobs.

"Can we see him?" Carol asked.

"The doctor told me just to bring the boy in."

"Yeah, I want to see him," Lucky said. He tried to wipe his tears away.

"Come with me," she said, and she smiled. Then she looked at Carol. "I'll take him in, and I'll see whether it's okay for you to come." She reached out for Lucky as he came around the desk, and the two walked in together.

When Lucky got to his dad's bed, he saw the difference. Dad had some color in his face. His eyes were open. But he still had all the tubes running into him, and he didn't move.

Lucky stepped close and said, "Hi, Dad." He wanted to stop crying, but he just couldn't.

His dad's eyes blinked, and his hand moved a little. Lucky reached out and took hold of the hand. "Are you okay?" Lucky asked.

Dad made a sound. With the tube in his mouth, he couldn't really speak, but Lucky knew he had tried to answer. And now it seemed real. Dad really was going to be all right.

"I've been . . . really worried," Lucky said, and the tears came fast again. He held his dad's hand tight, and he pushed his face against it, tears and all.

He held on for a long time. He knew his dad couldn't talk, and he knew he couldn't say much himself. So he just held Dad's hand to his face and whispered to God again, "Thank you. Thank you."

The nurse had disappeared. In a little while she came back. When Lucky looked up, he saw Carol. She stepped to the other side of the bed. Dad raised his hand a little and tried to reach for her, but the hand had an IV running into it.

She grasped his wrist. "I'm so relieved," she said, but like Lucky she couldn't get much out at all. She cried, and she clung to his arm. Dad looked at Carol, and then at Lucky, his eyes moving more than his head. He seemed to want to make contact with both of them.

And Lucky knew what Dad wanted to say. "I love you too, Dad," he whispered. Lucky looked at Carol, and the thought crossed his mind that his dad was right—Carol really was beautiful.

The next few days were difficult. Dad was recovering but only very slowly. Life in the neighborhood was anything but normal. People who hadn't taken too much damage tried to put things back together. Meanwhile, the aftershocks continued to make everyone very nervous. Grandma refused to put things back on the shelves for now.

Most people in the ward didn't dare move back into their homes. The dam had held, so the people from the river bottoms had been able to go home after one night. Electricity was still off in most areas of town, and that meant eating from storage or seventy-two-hour kits. Most people had enough that they could get by all right for a few weeks at least, but a lot of easy tasks had become complicated. Lucky was glad it wasn't the middle of winter.

Not many people were returning to work right away, and school couldn't start, so people spent their days repairing their houses, clearing away rubble, and telling their stories to each other.

Rebuilding was a slow process, what with so many people in the same situation, but families in the ward shared their food and their camping equipment and everything else.

Lucky went to the Hamptons' funeral, held at the ward chapel. The chapel was quite dark, and the microphone wouldn't work, but people were getting used to those things. Bishop Hess talked about them and their devotion to their neighbors and told the ward members, "I've seen you at your best these past few days. Tragedy, in and of itself, is not a blessing. But when we use tragedy to bring out the best in us, we can turn something like this into a blessing."

It was the sort of thing that Dad would say.

After the funeral, Lucky saw Carol and her family out in the foyer. He walked over to them, but he didn't know exactly what to say. Everything was so strange right now.

"Hi, Lucky," Kristin said. She smiled at him and then leaned close to his ear. "How's my little brother?" she whispered.

Lucky grinned and then shrugged, and as he looked around at Carol and the girls, he was pretty sure they had guessed what she had said. They were all smiling, looking happier than they had in a long time.

Lucky looked at Tyler. Lucky had seen him around a few times since that first day in the hospital, but Tyler had seemed embarrassed, as though he didn't know quite what to say.

Now he said, "Uh . . . do you want to do something?"

"I guess. I'm going down to the hospital in a little while."

Tyler nodded, shuffled his feet a little, and asked, "Do you want to come over to our place for a while?"

It was a peace offer, if ever there was one. "Okay," Lucky said, and Carol looked very pleased.

Lucky and Tyler walked down the hallway. Just outside they ran into Willy talking to Erin and Celeste.

"How's your dad doing?" Celeste asked.

"He's getting a little better every day. It's just really slow."

"I'm glad he's going to be all right though."

Erin said, "So what's the deal? Are you and Tyler going to be brothers now—as soon as your dad gets better?"

It was typical Erin—saying what most people wouldn't—but it didn't sound exactly like the old Erin. There was something softer in her tone.

Lucky glanced at Tyler. He didn't know what to say, but Tyler spoke up, "Maybe. We don't know for sure."

Erin wouldn't let him get away that easily. "Is that okay with you guys?"

If she had been teasing, Tyler and Lucky would probably have both told her it was none of her business. But she seemed serious.

Still, who was going to answer?

Lucky finally said, "I didn't like the idea at first, but it's okay with me now."

"Yeah," Tyler added, nodding.

Willy raised his hands in triumph, as though he somehow had something to do with it. "That'll make Kristin my stepcousin," he said. And then he grinned. "Kissin' cousins."

"You wish!" Erin said. And she sounded more like herself.

Tyler just shook his head, as if to say, Do I have to accept the cousin with this deal?

That afternoon Lucky walked to the hospital, the way he had done every day. Everyone seemed to be walking more these days—as though they all wanted to do things in ways they could depend on.

Dad was out of Intensive Care now and in his own room. The doctors had told him that his head injury had not developed into as serious a problem as they had feared. Mostly he just had to recover from the surgery and all the trauma to his body.

When Lucky walked into the room, Dad was sitting up. He looked more alert than he had the day before.

"How are you doing today?" Lucky asked.

"Good," Dad said. "I could beat you up. Easy."

Dad's voice, though weak, did sound firm.

"If you're so tough," Lucky replied, "get out of bed and try me."

Dad smiled—a little. He didn't laugh. Lucky doubted that he could crack off one of his big laughs right now. He just didn't have the strength.

"How's everyone doing?" Dad asked.

"Okay. We went to the funeral this morning. Just about everyone in the ward was over there."

"Was it nice?"

"Yeah. I guess. It wasn't really, really sad. Everyone seemed to have a good attitude about it—even the Hamptons' son and daughter. They were the speakers."

"That's how Mormon funerals are."

Lucky wondered about that. The only funeral he could compare was his mother's, and he could only remember aching at that one.

"Dad, Tyler and I talked to Erin today."

"So is she your new woman?"

"Come on, Dad."

"Well, what do you expect me to think? Everywhere we go, some new girl goes ga-ga over you."

"Ga-ga? What the heck is that?"

Dad did laugh a little, but then he had to wait for a few seconds before he could talk. "I can't laugh," he finally said. Then he added, "I thought you wanted to meet ol' Kaahu at college or something—and walk off into the sunset with her."

"Maybe I will," Lucky said, smiling.

"Won't you break Erin's heart? Or Celeste's? Or a dozen other girls'?"

"Not me. You're the one who makes women fall in love with you."

"Well, yeah, that's true. I seem to have something going for me. I'll have to admit that. Two really smart, beautiful women have fallen in love with me in my life."

"Carol *does* love you, Dad."

"I know that." And now he looked serious. "Is that okay with you?"

"That's what I was going to tell you. Erin asked me and Tyler if we were going to be brothers, and Tyler said maybe we were, and then she asked us if that was okay. I said it was, and so did Tyler."

Dad nodded, and tears came into his eyes. He didn't talk for quite some time, and when he did, his voice was still thick with emotion. "Isn't that just like us?" he said. "A darn earthquake knocks a house down on top of me—and it turns out to be my lucky break."

"Next time, could you catch a break some easier way?"

"Hey, I wasn't worried. I knew it was only a small house. When it all came down on me, before I lost consciousness, I said to myself, 'You've got to live, boy. You've got Lucky out there worrying about you.'"

"I was so scared, Dad." Lucky didn't want to cry again. He had done too much of that lately. But he didn't seem to have too much choice in the matter.

Dad waved him closer, and Lucky stepped to the side of the bed. Dad reached out and got an arm around him. "You're my blessing, Lucky. You always have been. I should have called you that instead of Lucky, but it would have sounded stupid, I guess. Blessed Ladd—or something like that."

Dad laughed a little, and then moaned, sort of making fun of the pain. Lucky laughed a little too, but he was also still crying.

"So let's stay here now, okay?" Dad said. "And let's have us a whole family and see how that goes? Is that all right with you?"

"Yeah."

"Of course, if I don't get up and around soon, Carol might find someone better."

"She could look everywhere in the world, Dad, but she wouldn't find anyone better." Lucky put his head against his dad's chest and really let go, his tears wetting his dad's hospital gown.

"Oh, Lucky, you're something," Dad said, and he laid his cheek against Lucky's head. Lucky could feel the warm tears seep into his hair. "No wonder everyone falls in love with you."

About the Author

When Dean Hughes was a kid, he dreamed that he would be a writer when he grew up. "Well," he says, "I accomplished the first part; I'm a writer. Now if I can just grow up."

The truth is, he doesn't try very hard at growing up. He spends his time writing kids' books, reading kids' books, and visiting schools to speak to kids. He's also a bishop, which keeps him involved with the youth in his ward.

Dean says about his writing, "Before I start a novel, I brainstorm. Then I work out an outline. I write many drafts of the book, sometimes nine or ten, before I'm satisfied. I do some of my writing while I run. Running is one of my favorite pastimes. While I jog, I process my writing ideas, working out problems and things like dialogue in my mind."

Dean has written over sixty books. He also skis and plays golf. He even ran a marathon some time ago, but he vowed never to do it again. So far he's been able to keep his vow.

He and his wife, Kathy, live in Provo, Utah. They have a married daughter, Amy, and two adult sons, Tom and Rob.

Have you read all the Lucky books?

Lucky's Crash Landing (#1). In California, Lucky learns how to skateboard the hard way. His new friends suspect he's an accident waiting to happen.

Lucky Breaks Loose (#2). In Louisiana, Lucky becomes football's smallest running back. Will he break loose for the long gain or break into little pieces?

Lucky's Gold Mine (#3). Lucky's adventures move to Montana, where he learns of an abandoned gold mine, and then has to stage a daring rescue there in the snow.

Lucky Fights Back (#4). In Massachusetts, Bunch is out to pound Lucky. If Lucky fights back, he'll become mincemeat. If he doesn't, he'll still become mincemeat.

Lucky's Mud Festival (#5). Towns have flooded along the Skagit River in Washington. Lucky decides to put on a mud festival to raise money for Christmas relief.

Lucky's Tricks (#6). Lucky returns to Provo, his hometown. He soons hears talk of marriage. Has Lucky's mother been forgotten? How can he get his dad to come to his senses?

Lucky the Detective (#7). In Kansas City, someone tries to break into the Ladds' mobile home. Lucky sets out to find the criminal.

Lucky's Cool Club (#8). In Woodland, Illinois, everyone looks and acts cool. But Lucky is about the uncoolest kid around. Even when he's invited to join a cool club, everyone drops out but Lucky.

Lucky in Love (#9). The Hawaiian sun has burned Lucky cherry red, and windsurfing wrecks have put bandages all over his face. Then he sees Kaahu. Unfortunately, she sees him too.